Good-Bye, Lover

Good-Bye, Lover

RACHEL BRITZ

To: Meredith
Here's to your
"Becoming" story!

AMBASSADOR INTERNATIONAL
GREENVILLE, SOUTH CAROLINA & BELFAST, NORTHERN IRELAND
www.ambassador-international.com

Good-Bye, Lover

ISBN: 978-1-62020-546-4
eISBN: 978-1-62020-454-2

Cover Design and Page Layout by Hannah Nichols
eBook Conversion by Anna Riebe Raats

AMBASSADOR INTERNATIONAL
Emerald House
427 Wade Hampton Blvd.
Greenville, SC 29609, USA
www.ambassador-international.com

AMBASSADOR BOOKS
The Mount
2 Woodstock Link
Belfast, BT6 8DD, Northern Ireland, UK
www.ambassadormedia.co.uk

The colophon is a trademark of Ambassador

DEDICATION

This story is dedicated to my children; Lily, Walker, and Perah.

No matter the struggle, God is with you.

No matter the fear, His covenant of peace will shelter you.

No matter the surrender, Love never fails. It does not end.

CHAPTER 1

COUNTY DONEGAL, IRELAND

1880

THE SECOND MOST IMPORTANT THING to Pop was Lover. Oh, she was a beauty—a treasure. Pop talked about her with a sparkle in his eye, the same way, I suppose, I overheard him talk about me, his first and only daughter, Honora Katherine Gallagher.

That's why I was surprised to notice that Lover was missing from her usual resting place on the mantel. *How odd.*

"Morning, my lady," Miss Pavek exclaimed as she scooted past the swinging kitchen door with a steaming plate of pancakes in her hand. "Are you ready for the big day?"

"Indeed," I looked around the empty great room. "Has the bride-to-be made an appearance?"

"Heavens no, that'd be dreadfully unlucky. Besides, I doubt the girl slept a wink. I think she finished her duties before the sun split the sky." Miss Pavek shook her head as she set the plate on the table.

"I think this is quite possibly my favorite day of the year!"

"Aye, you and the whole of Ireland." Miss Pavek stopped to cinch the apron strings around her thimble-like waist before escaping through the revolving door.

Shrove Tuesday. The last day to indulge before the forty days of Lent began. Today was a day to feast, which is why, I presume, it's become the most favored day to host a wedding celebration.

My stomach ached with that hollow feeling that bespoke of hunger or angst, I wasn't sure which. I couldn't help but stare at the gaping space on the mantel.

On a normal day, silvery clouds wrapped themselves around the castle like a thin coat; however, today was not a normal day. The peculiar sun leaking through the room's tall, stone-arched windows shifted my attention and I noticed all the servants bustling with activity in the courtyard below. Surely, the sunshine was a sign of good fortune for my dear friend—best friend, actually—Angela. Our bond was a bond few understood because of our differences.

"You need to be mindful," Pop had warned. "We have a tradition to uphold."

Kings Castle—my home, proudly nestled along the River Eske on the outskirts of town—towered with a simple elegance, like the nearby coastal cliffs that had been sculpted by the spirited sea and wind. My Pop had always been eager to build a home. I once overheard him say that when Grandda passed, he left a small inheritance to each of his four boys. Only the eldest son, my Uncle Donahue, received the family estate, a manner house in Waterford. So while the other two brothers took their fortunes and immigrated to America, well, when Pop received this abandoned castle and several plots of land from a distant uncle, he took his father's inheritance and my Mam—swollen with pregnancy—and moved far away from home to this castle. Pop definitely was the ambitious type! He called this their new beginning.

But above all else, my Pop had sought to forge a reputation that was renowned for taking care of the people, our community. From the rich to the poor, and the landowner to the tenant: "'Tis all God's people dat are created equally," my Pop would boast. This would become a virtuous message ingrained into the fiber of my being, and I suppose that's why Pop never said Angela and I couldn't be friends. Nevertheless, she was a servant; so, for as long as I can remember, Angela and I have tucked our friendship away like a secret diary.

I speared a pancake from the tall stack.

"Ah-hem." A planked floorboard creaked behind my seat. "Did you forget something, my lady?" *That strict voice. Miss Celia.* I rolled my eyes.

"My apologies." I dropped the cake onto my plate and grabbed my table napkin, spreading it across my lap. *Manners, manners, manners . . .* Seventeen years of rhythmic instruction echoed in my mind.

"Grace . . . ?"

Huh? I turned toward Miss Celia and my face stiffened, mirroring hers.

"Did you say grace, Honora?" Her lips pursed as she spoke.

Nora. I wish she'd simply call me Nora, like everyone else. Biting my lip, I fought the urge to speak my mind once and for all. Instead, as commanded, I closed my eyes and bowed my head, but I couldn't help the rotten image that passed through my mind: Miss Celia with a heap of burning coals upon her head. *I'm a horrible person for such a thought. I just wish she would stop mothering me and let me be!* When would she trust that she had raised me right and true according to the standards by which every proper young lady learned the art of deportment? Not only that, but also that she'd raised me right and true according to the Gallagher standards? Soon, I'd be old enough to govern my own life—a day I've dreamed of many times. In a year I'd be eighteen years old, and free. Or so I hoped.

But, as much as she's tried, Miss Celia could never replace my Mam. *Mam was dead.*

I had to switch my thoughts before tears burned my eyes. I completed my frustrated grief by skewering Miss Celia with a glare.

"Do you know where my Pop is?" I couldn't stave my hunger any longer. I picked up my fork and smeared butter across my golden cake. Alas, my mouth was watering. "Today, of all days . . . I thought he'd surely beat the crow to breakfast."

"Indeed"—a rare smile parted Miss Celia's thin lips—"yer Pop loves pancake day! He'll be arriving as soon as he finishes up some affairs." Miss Celia took a step back and tilted her head to get a better view of the courtyard. "He should be joining you shortly," her voice faded.

I followed Miss Celia's stare and saw Pop conversing with a man near the castle gate. They shook hands and began to exchange—*Ach! What was Pop doing?*

My chair banged to the floor as I stood with more speed than when I dressed on a cold winter's morn. I gripped the edge of the table with white-knuckled hands as my father handed the wooden case containing Lover to this—*Oh, wait, it was only Jack.*

I slunk back into my seat before I had a chance to swallow my sticky pancake. Jack Griffith, the Traveling Tinker, was often hired by Pop for a variety of tasks, but mainly to tend to Lover when it came to measures of maintenance such as rosining the bow, changing her strings, and polishing when necessary. More so, the very thing I'd grown to appreciate about Mr. Griffith was his musical talent. Despite my best efforts at winning this title, Jack Griffith was the best fiddle player in the county.

"Honora Gallagher, what has gotten into you? Now, stop worrying long enough to finish yer breakfast. Lover will be returned to her rightful place in a wee bit."

In town, behind Agee's Tweed & Fashion, I carefully followed the crooked steps leading to Angela's home, a rented space tucked beneath the shop. I knocked once and then pushed open the thick wooden door. Mag O'Sheen and Mary Ellen McCourt huddled around the bride. The two of them, wives of tenant farmers and residents on land owned by the castle, were always together. They supported the community with their midwifery skills, as it was typically Mag and Mary Ellen who were called upon when preparations for a birth or burial were needed. In fact, it was Mag who helped my Mam deliver me into this world. *That same fateful day of her death.* But I couldn't think about Mam now. Not today. Not on Angela's wedding day, a day worth celebrating. I just had to remember that today, Mag and Mary Ellen were simply helping Angela prepare for her wedding.

An oblong mirror in the corner of the room, turned dressing room, reflected Angela's bright smile. "Angela, you are the most beautiful bride I've ever seen!" I wanted to skip like a happy little girl on the best day of her life. Today she would marry John O'Doolan. Technically, both were servants to our estate, but to me, they were John and Angela, my friends. John held the position of handling all the trades for the castle by ordering supplies and orchestrating the sale of goods. Angela was our housemaid and castle seamstress. The two were a grand pair.

I stared at Angela's dress. It was two pieces: a long skirt that hugged her waist, flowing to the floor, and the top was a fitted suit coat tailored to her petite shoulders.

Mag's mouth dropped, as did the handful of Angela's curls she'd been holding.

"Lady Nora, what in the world are you doing down here?" She tried to hush her deep, groveled voice.

"I know, Mag. 'Tis not very proper to be barging in like this but I couldn't help myself. I needed to see Angela before the Mass." Proper formalities would keep our public conversation limited, and I couldn't wait until the wee dancing hour to share in her excitement.

"Shouldn't *you* be getting ready?" Mag looked me up and down.

"I *am* ready." I brushed a hand across my pale gray skirt. I do suppose it wasn't the fanciest ensemble in my wardrobe.

"Surely, my lady, Miss Celia didn't see you leaving the castle dressed like that?"

"This skirt has special meaning to me. Angela made it for me." I smiled.

Mag shrugged and then finished pinning the final strands of Angela's hair in place.

"Besides, I've come only for a brief moment to wish my dear fr . . . umm, favorite seamstress a grand day."

Angela twirled to face me.

"I can't believe you designed your very own wedding gown." I reached to touch the shimmering arm of her suit coat. "I've never seen a color like this."

"Charles Worth calls it Oyster Pearl." Angela's voice seemed to squeal in jubilation.

"So this is the fabric you chose from *the* Charles Worth pamphlet?" Since Angela lived beneath Agee's clothing shop, she was privy to see fashion advertisements from all over the world. We'd long declared that the elaborate French designer was our favorite. One day I hoped to take Angela to his Paris shop; in the meantime, she fared well enough copying Worth's reputable dresses.

"Aye." Angela leaned towards me and whispered, "If it wasn't for your generosity . . . Lord knows, we'd never be able to afford such costly fabric."

"There, there. You're going to make me blush. Besides, who wouldn't want to give her best friend a grand gift on her wedding day? You can thank my father, but it was our delight." I turned my head and saw Mag's eyebrow rise while she reached to primp Angela's hair. If there was a gossip column in *The Examiner* I knew that our costly gift would likely make next week's headline.

I heard a muffled cough from the corner of the windowless room and turned to see Angela's frail mother sitting in a chair. She held a needle in one hand, and was busily stitching from a pile of lace on her lap.

"Oh! Hello, Mrs. McGowan. You've been so quiet, I didn't even notice you."

Angela's Ma kept her head down and paid no mind to my greeting.

"She can't hear you," Angela explained. "First it was her eyesight. Now the hearing is going too."

"I'm sorry, Angela. It's amazing that she can still work a needle and thread."

Angela laughed. "Don't fool yourself. Ma was practically born holding a needle, and I'm sure she'll go to the grave with one too."

"Sounds like someone else I know." I smiled.

Angela giggled, "I think she's quite determined to make her baby girl's wedding veil. I suppose I can't fault her for that."

I thought about my Mam and wondered if she too enjoyed sewing. The only thing I really knew about her was how much she had loved playing the fiddle. Sometimes I thought about all those little things. *What did her voice sound like? What color was her hair? Was it thick and unruly? Did she have skin that was fair and lightly freckled like mine?* The only memories I held were the few Miss Celia, Mag, and occasionally my Pop shared with me.

A loud pounding on the door caused everyone, including Mrs. McGowan, to jump.

"Fancy that," Mag puffed as she watched Miss Celia enter.

"Whew. For a moment I thought the Strawboys were about to crash the wedding," Angela sighed.

"The day isn't over yet." I smiled. Everyone knew the Strawboys could show up at any moment on your wedding day. Those uninvited folks gleaned any opportunity to masquerade in straw hats and costumes and attempt to steal the bride away from her groom. It was all in good fun, but nonetheless, Angela desired to avoid any such escapade.

"There you are, my lady. I've been searching for you all over town! Yer Pop is waiting to escort you to the wedding." Miss Celia briefly glanced around the room. "Angela," she nodded, her lips famously pursed. An awkward tension seemed to squeeze the air from the room.

Mag's jaw stiffened. "Well, ain't she miss high and mighty," she muffled under her breath as she rummaged through her leather tote.

"Yes, well, I was just bidding—"

Miss Celia glared at Mag but spoke to me. "You'll have plenty of time for that. Now, we'd best hurry or you'll have no time to change out of those rags."

Angela passed a quick, empathetic glance my way. Why must Miss Celia care so much about my appearance? Soon, I'd be old enough to choose my own style. And in the same spirit I was going to further my education in music. The music school in Dublin awaited me. I only needed Pop's blessing.

Pop stood at the bottom of the stairs in the vaulted entryway waiting to escort me to John and Angela's wedding ceremony.

"Nora! You're lookin' beautiful." Pop's stout face glowed. "Me wee gissa is growin' up before me very eyes."

"Oh Pop." I made my way down the stairway, gripping the banister so as to not trip on the lace dust ruffle hemmed to the bottom of my purple gown. It had been Miss Celia's selection, naturally.

"It's bound to happen." I shrugged. It seemed simple, to me. When you grow up, you pursue your dreams—if you're able. I was fully aware that most women my age were not afforded such luxury, but we were fortunate. Pop's hard work to establish himself in the community as a trustworthy landowner and God-fearing man had earned him the position he deserved and awarded me with additional opportunities.

"What's bound to happen?" Pop inquired as he lifted his chin and rocked onto his toes— his vain attempt at adding measure to his height. A measure, might I add, that I'd slightly surpassed.

"Your wee gissa, growing up and going off to pursue her dream."

Pop frowned. I noticed his chest deflate like a balloon. "Aye. I see. Dat dream again."

I peered through the open archway leading into the great room. I couldn't help but imagine. I fixed my gaze, wishing I could see the mantel from my position.

"What is it?" Pop looked awkwardly over his shoulder.

"Do you think we could bring Lover with us to the wedding? I know how much it pains you to allow her to leave the castle. It's only . . . this is an extremely special day. I was thinking I might be able to play a jig or two at this evening's craic. That is, if you'd allow it this one time. Oh Pop, *please* say yes."

"Nora, you know how I feel." Pop's mouth sagged like a willowy branch. "If anything ever happened . . . "

"I know, Pop. Lover is worth a lot of money and I swear on my life that I'll take good care of her."

"Me gissa, is dat what you think this is about? The money? The value Lover possesses is far greater than what meets the eye. When your mother and I came to Kings Castle all those years ago, we didn't have much in way of possessions . . . except for Lover. During nights when we longed for home, your mother would pick up her beloved family fiddle and play. It's all I have left of her," he explained.

I watched the color in Pop's cheeks flush as he spoke. It was rare for Pop to speak of Mam. Perhaps, it was too difficult. But for the first time I felt as though I was hearing an honest confession about why he adored Lover the way he did. It made my appreciation grow deeper. I was silent.

"Now, as you've grown, I see so much of her in you." Pop sighed. "Hurry now, go fetch Lover or we'll be late for the wedding."

I gasped with giddy delight and hugged Pop as if I might never see him again. Then I sprung to the great room to pluck my fiddle from the mantel.

"Come along, me sunshine of my heart." Pop beckoned me in a lyrical outburst.

Sunshine. Princess sunshine. Sunshine of my heart. All terms used by Pop whenever he called upon me, his one and only daughter, Honora Katherine Gallagher. *Sunshine of The Heart* was a ballad by Ireland's Samuel Lover, and one of Pop's favorite composers.

As we stepped out into the courtyard, Thomas our driver was positioned in front of the jaunting car adjusting the bridle on our lead horse, Snow. Pop looped his arm in mine as he walked me around the side of the carriage.

"Thank you, Pop. I promise to take good care of Lover." Pop patted my arm as he steadied my balance while I took my seat. I loved the short ride into town, especially on days like today when the sun shone and the skies opened bright. Pop took his seat next to me, Lover secure between the two of us.

"May I play a tune while we ride?" I felt a strange sensation in my chest. My heart began to flutter as if a butterfly were beating its wings for the first time. Slow, dreamy. I wanted to share once more my desire to go off to Dublin and play my music. But what if Pop said no, again?

"Dat would be delightful, Nora."

I pulled Lover from her case and tucked her beneath my chin like I'd done so many times before. As I slid the bow across the tight strings, my eyes shuttered closed. The fiddle seemed to leak a soft tune, slow at first. I began to sway. The sound of Snow's clomping hooves beat in rhythm with the song. As we picked up pace I felt a light breeze swirl around my face, down my neck and shoulders, tickling my arms and into my fingertips. The warm sun on my face fueled the song pouring out of my heart. The stroke of my bow in a back and forth motion made me feel as though I were painting the wind with emotional colors of joy and peace.

When I finally opened my eyes, I realized we'd arrived at the church.

"Dat was beautiful." Pop beamed. "I'm certain your Mam is beamin' down upon you."

"She really loved music as much as I?"

"Aye, it was in her blood. When I look at you and the young woman you're becoming, I can't help but see her in you."

"Pop?" I placed Lover back in her case and began to fidget with the clasp. "I'd like to request your permission . . . " Pop blanketed me with his undivided attention and I could feel my anxiousness climb like the sprawling ivy along the castle's southern wall. It would be easier to contain my emotions if I didn't look into Pop's eyes so I occupied my gaze upon the wooden case. "When I come of age next year, I'd like to go to Dublin and take up my studies at the Herbert School of Music."

Pop sat real still. The silence gnawed at me like a beetle on bark.

"I don't understand, Nora. A proper lady your age ought to consider gettin' married, aye? I've built a perfect life for you here at Kings Castle. Why do you feel the need to go so far away from me when you can play music *here*? I could hire another—"

"Forgive me, father. I want to respect your decision but do you understand how important this is to me? You said that music was in Mam's blood and if I'm living proof of her existence then you should want to see these dreams fulfilled."

"Of course! You are the Sunshine of my Heart." Pop reached for my hand, squeezing it real tight. "I can see your determination and I'm trying to understand."

Taking a deep breath he said, "I leave for a trip tomorrow, but upon my return we shall discuss making the proper arrangements."

CHAPTER 2

MISS CELIA BURST INTO MY room while the moon hung in the black night. I gasped, sitting straight up, my eyes focusing on her shadow moving toward me.

"Come quickly," she exclaimed, her breath pushing through clenched teeth.

I watched as her elongated figure trailed out the doorway, and as abruptly as she came, she was gone.

I tore away my covers and jumped out of bed. My legs were shaking as I grabbed the wooden pollster of my bed for stability. A myriad of fuzzy thoughts ran through my mind.

My fingers nervously fumbled with the ties of my robe. My breaths were short and nervous—the kinds one struggles with when anticipating someone jumping at them from out of the darkness. As I walked down the hallway, a soft glow from the flaming wall sconces illuminated the spiral staircase. I could hear faint voices echoing from the great room below. Slipping my fingers over the polished banister, I trailed my hand down it on my way to the bottom of the stairs.

As my eyes began to adjust in the dimly lit room, the moon cast shadows on a handful of people scattered among the room.

Something was wrong. Dreadfully wrong. I could sense the presence of anguish like the chest-crushing weight of horrible news. The sensation filled the room like a steam-induced sweathouse. Constable Red O'Riley stood erect in the center of the room, tall and bull-necked. His thick, weathered hand reached to straighten the patch covering his eye. Miss Celia perched at his side, her thin lips nearly erased. Pinched. She knew something that I was not privy to.

"What's going on? What aren't you telling me? Please. Someone say something!" I pressed my shoulders back bracing for the worst. "Will someone speak!"

Miss Celia fidgeted with her hands, "'Tis yer Pop. The most vile news . . . " She bit her cheek and squeezed her eyes shut.

"O'Riley?" I questioned. My pulse quickened and my heart threatened to beat itself right out of my chest.

"There's been an incident," O'Riley began as if someone dragged the words from his mouth. "Your Pop was returning from his travels to Glenties and was ambushed." He turned to look towards the darkened corner of the great room. There I noticed our castle's young driver, Thomas, hugging himself so tight his knuckles appeared purple.

"Thomas was driving the cart when the attack happened . . . but he managed to flee on horseback."

"I—I don't understand. Where is my Pop?" I looked at Miss Celia, her head hung like a willowy branch.

"He was killed, my lady. I'm terribly sorry."

Out of the corner of my eye I noticed Thomas begin to sway. *An attack?*

"What? Who did this?" I marched up to Thomas who was visibly distressed. "How can you be sure, boy?" But he just stood there, shaking. Miss Celia came, wrapped her arms around my shoulders and turned me around. Mag appeared and led Thomas out of the room through the kitchen door.

O'Riley's face showed no emotion. How could he be so put together? *Nearly twenty years of working day in and day out with my Pop, and this? How could he be so stoic?* If I didn't know any better, I'd think O'Riley was a cold-hearted man. Except, I knew better. There was only one man my Pop trusted to manage the affairs of this castle, and that was Red O'Riley. He'd been around long enough and involved in enough for me to witness his heart.

"I've notified Leo to increase security at the castle gate, as well as the local garda to track down these criminals and, uh, . . . rescue the remains of . . ." With that last phrase, his official tone broke.

In that eclipsed moment, I became a stranger to my surroundings. The comfort of what was the rightful placement of everything that belonged to me was stripped bare. It seemed as if every movement and motion slowed. I nodded, as if in agreement, but I had no comprehension of what O'Riley was saying to me.

Numbness washed over me and I needed to excuse myself. As I closed the door to my bedchamber, a heavy chill in the air pressed against my skin. *How could this be?* I looked around my perfectly square room: my sugan chair positioned in the corner near my writing desk, and the tall chestnut wardrobe standing regal against the wall. All my belongings were in their proper place, and yet, it felt as if I was standing in the middle of an empty room. The vacancy seemed to echo in my pounding head. Pop had always called this room my "keep," like the castle. He said it was made for my safekeeping, but I didn't feel very safe tonight. I wandered over and stood in front of my window, staring into blackness. Somewhere beyond that pitch of night, the Bluestack Mountains spread across the eastern horizon. I wouldn't believe it if I hadn't grown up seeing it.

And I wouldn't believe my Pop was dead until I could see him with my very own eyes.

My lip began to quiver. I staggered over to my bed and collapsed, burying my face into my feather pillow until I was forced to gasp for air. Any sense of understanding seemed lost. Overwhelmed and surprised by a most terrifying fear, I curled up in a ball and wept. *How could this happen to such a good man? Who would take care of me? What would become of Kings Castle and all the people that depended upon us for survival?* Question upon question rolled in like fog. A surge of tears soaked my pillow.

A knock at the door disturbed my thoughts. Miss Celia entered, walked silently towards me, and sat down at the foot of my bed.

"I've taken the liberty to summon Mag and Mary Ellen."

"Whatever for?"

"We'll need them to make the preparations for burial."

"Already? I mean, shouldn't we wait until we know for sure? What if Thomas was wrong and Pop isn't dead after all?" A hint of anger nipped at my words.

Miss Celia swallowed hard, "My dear," she patted my arm with a strange affection, "the garda have just arrived with his body."

Pop had been laid out on the wooden table near the window. As I entered the great room I covered my mouth. His eyes were closed, the pallor of his skin gray, cold . . . dead. Pop's florid hair was brushed back from his forehead, but I could see, I knew, that it hid a gash in his head. I shook my head. *Was this really happening?* I ran my hand across the smooth white linen sheet that was draped over his body. Without thinking, I began tucking and folding the sheet under the lifeless weight of his body.

Oh, Pop!

I thought of the countless times he tucked me into bed at night. "You're the Sunshine of my Heart," he would proclaim. It felt as if I could hear him humming that tune right now.

I walked over to Mag and Mary Ellen who quietly stood at the end of the table.

"Thank you for taking such grand care of him." My eyes burned as they filled with tears again.

"We're deeply troubled by this senseless loss, my lady." Mary Ellen gently rubbed the top of my hand with her frail fingertips.

"Do you have any idea who would commit such an atrocity?" Mag huffed. "It's rumored to be one of those secret societies and let me tell you, I've had just about enough of those troublemakers going around . . . " Mary Ellen yanked Mag's arm.

"And whatever you need from us, please, do not hesitate to ask," Mary Ellen interrupted. "We'll be here through the waking."

Mag blotted the corners of her tired-looking eyes and turned away.

I don't know why I was surprised that rumors of the tragedy were already spreading like wildfire. It was Donegal Town after all; a town that by its very nature produced its share of headlines each month when the Fair Day market rolled into the town's Diamond, the open square located in the center of town.

I looked around the room and noticed a few servants standing guard and conversing in small pods.

"Have you seen Angela?" I asked Miss Celia who was busily opening all the windows. Several years ago when my Grandmam passed away, we traveled to my Pop's family home in Waterford. I watched the ladies get all the preparations in order, insistent on opening the windows to ward off evil spirits, so I imagined that's what Miss Celia was doing.

"She's with John, they're returning from a trade in Killybegs."

"Does she know?" I gulped.

"Indeed," Miss Celia nodded, "a messenger was sent. I expect their return this evening."

My stomach growled.

"Have you eaten something today?"

I shook my head.

"Go, get a bite. Today will be a long day and you'll be needing every bit of energy. I've also laid out yer mourning dress for you."

Miss Celia struck a match and lit a small candle; it flickered as she placed it on the edge of the open window. "You'd best hurry. Father Reed, Mr. Griffith, and the hired keener are on their way to begin the waking."

Frank O'Sheen, Mag's husband and caretaker of the livery, approached us through the swell of people beginning to overtake the great room.

"I hate to bother ya, my lady." Frank tipped his hat squishing his dark, shiny hair. "I was wondering if ya wouldn't mind coming with me to the stable for a moment."

"What's the bother, Frank?"

"It's Snow."

My Connemara pony. I remembered the day I witnessed her tiny thoroughbred form slip onto the earth. It was early spring, when I was still a wee one—that same year it snowed in sheets—and it had been love at first sight.

Not Snow, please, not Snow . . .

"It's okay. She's going to be fine, I think. It's just . . . since her return, she's not settling down. She won't let the boys or I come near without her causing a fuss. I thought, perhaps, your touch might calm her."

I followed Frank through the kitchen door, and I noticed Miss Pavek and the other cooks busy making food as we entered. Simmering pots billowed steam from the open fire. The scent of herbs and slow cooked lamb discretely caught my senses and made my insides feel like revolting. My stomach felt as though it had been trampled by a stampede of horses.

The long kitchen felt open because of its high, cedar-planked ceilings. In the center of the room, a butcher block table served a dual purpose: preparing food for daily meals, as well as the dining table for our servants. Along the far back wall, in the left corner was a small door that opened to a spiral staircase that led to the cellar—a place I'd never been, on purpose. Along the right side was a small arched door that routed through the pantry and out into the courtyard.

Stepping towards me, Miss Pavek stood upon her tiptoes and gave me a passionate hug.

"I can't believe it," she sniffed. With her handkerchief she rubbed the tip of her rosy nose. "Please sit and have a cup of tea. Can I get you something to eat?"

"Nae." I wrapped my arms around my waist. "Thank you, but we're just passing through." I looked at Frank who tugged on his suspenders with nervous energy. He shrugged. Frank wouldn't force me to do anything, but, who could eat at a time like this?

Miss Pavek shook her head and turned back to her work. There were no words. Disbelief had washed over her too.

As Frank escorted me through the pantry I noticed several cakes of freshly baked Fadge, a flat potato bread, cooling on top of the dark walnut countertops. Shelves containing bags of flour, tea, and other necessities stretched to the ceiling and lined both sides of the room. This is where Miss Pavek churned butter, and also happened to be my favorite place to escape. If only I could curl up in the corner of this pantry, maybe then I'd be able to get away from this nightmare. We ducked under the arched door at the far end of the pantry and stepped outside. Bits of gravel crunched beneath my feet as we passed the chicken byre and made our way to the corner stable. I looked around, taking in the flurry of activity that consumed the courtyard. As O'Riley suggested, a brood of fully armed garda lined the perimeter gate.

"Are we in some sort of danger?" I asked Frank, pointing towards the gunmen posted in the corner tower.

"Ya can never be too careful, my lady. Especially, when the likes of those crazy . . . "

"The likes of who?"

Frank removed his hat and rubbed his brow. "I don't mean to alarm ya, but they haven't arrested those responsible."

"Oh." A powerful gust of sea-air whipped against my face and sucked the breath from my lungs, forcing my eyes shut. How worse could it get? I felt a spark of anger ignite in my chest.

"What are we going to do?"

Frank leaned forward. "I overheard O'Riley and Leo talking quietly behind the gatekeeper's quarters. I could get only bits and pieces. They didn't want to tell ya because they thought it'd be best. No one wants ya to worry, but, I think ya ought to know. This is *your* castle now, after all."

My castle. Nae, it wasn't my castle. It was my Pop's. The one he'd worked hard to restore.

The sound of a loud whinny bugled from the corner stall and I jumped.

Snow.

Moving closer, I noticed Frank's boys flanked on either side of Snow. Junior and Paddy were the stable boys, helping their father manage the livery. I watched as Junior struggled with the lead rope while Paddy ignorantly waved his hands in front of Snow.

"Boys," Frank yelled, "come here." As Junior managed to secure the rope to the post, I noticed Snow's tongue drooped out of the side of her mouth. *That's odd.* Nonetheless, the further the boys moved away from her, the calmer she appeared.

"Is she injured?" I asked as I slowly walked towards her.

"She has a small cut on the side of her face. Nothing that won't heal." Frank looked at me empathetically.

I reached to touch Snow's forehead and she instantly jolted. "There, there girl," I whispered.

"But, what's wrong with her tongue?"

"Ya, sure. My guess is it's transient paralysis. This would make sense if she experienced trauma to the side of her face, which appears to be consistent with her injury. I'm going to give it a few days, monitor her pain, and make sure she is able to eat and drink. I'm sure time will heal."

Trauma to the side of her face. The image of Pop sprang into my mind. I swallowed hard to suppress my unruly emotions. "I can't believe this—How did this happen anyway?" The question forced all the breath from my chest.

"Ya, right now Thomas is the only witness. He's a bit shaken so the details are spotty." Frank winced.

A single blast, followed by a scream, exploded from the courtyard. Snow reared her head and her ears laid back at the sound.

We ran outside and I saw a plume of smoke rising from near the castle gate. Red O'Riley was shouting at a man in uniform.

A growing number of people, including myself, converged to get a closer look. What was happening? Just then I felt a hand squeeze my arm and jerk me away from the crowd. I was pulled so hard it made my head spin, and my face smashed into the fold of a blue uniformed chest. The man gripped my shoulders as he moved, and I felt like a stringed puppet being dragged across a stage. I took my fists and shoved the man as hard as I could. As he stumbled backwards, I saw his face and I realized it was Leo—our gatekeeper and Red O'Riley's eager apprentice.

"What do you think you're doing?" I sighed, brushing myself off for measure.

"We've got this under control. You don't need to worry . . . "

"Worry? You don't know the least of my worries." I groaned, turning back to see that, in fact, everything was under control. Red O'Riley was wagging his finger and mouthing something to another castle guard wearing a blue uniform.

"I'm fine, Leo," I lied. I looked across the courtyard where five stone cottages lined themselves in a precise row, each a home to one of our servant families. The John and Angela O'Doolan cottage was dark. *When would they return?* I was desperate for Angela's company.

"I was only trying to protect you," Leo said.

I shook my head and began to amble towards the castle. That's when I heard a faint sound. The soft cadence lilted slowly, the way I imagine a leaf floats to earth on the morning breeze. The unimaginable sound of mourning was causing my skin to prickle. *Had it started already?* I turned my ear as the wailing sound repeated again and again, each time stronger and more distinct than before. The gentle murmur escalated to a full-scale tone, then fell to silence.

As it fell silent, I continued inside the castle, and found the great room had swollen with people. I watched as Jack Griffith held Lover beneath his chin, swaying to the sorrowful rhythm. Mag and Mary Ellen gave way to weeping loudly, their hands waving and pounding upon their chests. The undisturbed demeanor of the professional keener stood out to me. From the corner of the room, he occasionally joined the chorus with his deep guttural tone. *Was this really happening?* Indeed, it was; the waking song was underway, and I reckoned that soon all of Heaven would be acquainted with our grief.

CHAPTER 3

THE DARK SKIES THREATENED RAIN during Father Reed's blessing. Miss Celia and the other servants huddled together; their faces were pale, downcast, and wet. Their wide-eyed stares made me wonder if I looked as confused as they did. Standing there in that circle around the disturbed earth, we would say our final good-byes.

My heart sank and I forced myself to turn away. These people were like family to me. Since I had no brothers or sisters, these people were the only family I'd ever really known. But with the exception of myself, Pop had no *real* family members present at his funeral.

My red cloak hung over my shoulders. It felt thick and heavy, like the April air that filled my chest. I looked down at my black, patent leather clogs and thought about their faithfulness. Despite any likelihood of rain, I could trust they would keep me dry, like always. *Faithfulness.* The same message that Father Reed preached during Pop's eulogy. I hadn't cried throughout the service until he used *that* word to describe my father's character. It was true. But when Father Reed began to babble on about God's faithfulness to each one of us in our time of sorrow, it felt like someone kicked me in the stomach. *If God were faithful and good, why would He take my Pop away?* This wasn't fair. I swallowed; the sensation of a hot flame seeming to lick away at my insides.

The aroma of fresh dirt swirled in the air over Milmount Cemetery, a sacred land dedicated to all God-fearing people, regardless of religion. Mam was buried here. And now, rightfully so, a hole had been dug for Pop to rest in peace beside her. I surveyed the grassy hillside dotted with the accumulation of engraved stones and the line of well-wishers that stretched down the hill toward the old bridge crossing into downtown Donegal Town. Under normal circumstances, the marketplace would be bustling with activity, but today the streets looked more like an abandoned village.

I turned my attention to the pine box about to be lowered into the earth by a few servants. I knelt down to touch it. Saying good-bye was so final, and there was such a loneliness here. *How could this be?*

After Father Reed made his final remarks, I was invited to share a few words of respect to those in attendance. Miss Celia said it was the proper thing to do. *What did she understand about being put on the spot?* Absolutely nothing. Perhaps that's why it was easy for her to dictate how I should behave. But I'd honor her advice this time, for Pop.

All I know is that seeing the crowd of people encircled around me like a pack of thirsty pups caused me to sweat. I wanted to say the right thing, to reassure them that everything would be okay . . . *but how could it be?* As I started to speak, it felt like a bucket of words was being drawn from the well of my inner being.

"On this day, we celebrate the life of John Patrick Gallagher." The sound of my voice seemed to raise an octave. "Over the years, I presume many of you have been touched by his generosity. Pop celebrated all of you; whether you were a tenant, a member of his church, or partial to his work serving those in need. It's fair to say our community will deeply mourn his loss. As for myself and for those serving the castle, we are grateful for your love and support during this sorrowful time. I assure you with complete confidence that justice will be served to whomever was responsible for John Gallagher's death." I paused to catch my breath. "You have my word that the legacy of Kings Castle will live on. We will press on and continue the good work that my Pop worked tirelessly to establish. This is my word to you. And may God's favor be upon us all." I bowed my head and closed my eyes, fighting off the urge to run. It was like I was stuck in a bad dream, trying to flee from a vicious monster but unable to move.

Suddenly, I heard the slow, dramatic pitch of a bow slipping across the strings of a fiddle. My eyes flung open. Standing alone on the side of the hill, I caught a glimpse of Jack Griffith with Lover nestled beneath his chin. His tailored suit, smoky and gray like the looming clouds, was weathered and worn. The rim of his peaked cap pulled over his ears as he continued to play, leading the mass of people in procession. I wanted to march over to him and relish in his company, but grief was destroying my ambition and it felt as though my feet were stuck in a bog field.

The movement of people slowly leaving the cemetery grounds pushed me to begin the somber return home. Mr. Griffith's song began to fade as we moved further away. I glanced at the crowd of faces in front of me. For years this community had depended upon Kings Castle to supply jobs, coordinate trades, and advocate for the affairs of the less fortunate. Who would take up such a task now? It scared me when I thought about the enormity of it all. Surely, O'Riley would direct me since he was most privy to managing the castle affairs.

A hand slipped through my arm, and Angela hugged my side as we walked.

"This is awful. Your Pop was so kind and gracious to me and my family." Angela blotted the corner of her eyes with her handkerchief.

I nodded, "I still can't believe this is happening."

"We'll get through this. I mean, I don't know how, but . . . oh God, why?" Angela's lip began to quiver. I looked away. I needed to stay strong. I don't know why or for whom. Perhaps I felt the need to stay strong for everyone else.

As we approached the main gate, tenant farmers and their families had lined both sides of the narrow path. The local garda flanked both sides of the entrance allowing access only to special members of Pop's various committees, the church, and those serving the castle. I passed through the solid cedar door and noticed O'Riley positioned in front of the gatehouse—the small barrack that occupied the left side of the courtyard. That square building was made entirely of stone and was designed to store weapons and supplies, but it also served as a tactical meeting place, and as the lodging quarters for Leo and Thomas. As he stood there, O'Riley's expression was again stoic. Next to O'Riley, Leo stood at attention. Leo's smile usually exposed his dimple, but today was different; the dimple in his cheek appeared to be more sunken than usual, and he looked wounded. He clenched his jaw as if he were biting back pain.

My stomach did a somersault as I looked at them. I guess I wasn't the only one grieving.

As we entered the courtyard, the castle looked different. It appeared so much bigger today—so much larger than life.

In the great room, Miss Pavek, along with three other maiden cooks, stood along the back wall. The whole room had been transformed into one large reception hall. Tables covered in white linen lined the center of the room, candles glowed, and freshly baked bread, creamy potato soup, platters of cheese, warm pies, and butterprints adorned the buffet table.

"Here, let's get you dry." Angela tugged at the shoulder of my coat.

"Huh?" I fumbled with my unstable arms.

Angela held my face in her hands and spoke directly, "I'll be right back. I'm going to fetch you a warm jacket."

"Oh. Thank you."

I turned my head and noticed the room pulsed with well-wishers, many of whom were strangers to me. O'Riley motioned me over to the head of the growing reception line.

As he turned to face me, his broad shoulders blocked my view of the room and others around us.

"Are you well enough to conclude paying respects, my lady? You know, I can handle this if you feel the urge to seek rest."

I shook my head slightly. "I need to stay. Even though there are so many people here that I don't even recognize."

"Aye, a great deal have traveled quite the distance to be here today. No worry, I shall introduce you. But afterwards, assure me that you'll retreat for a bit. We've got things under control."

For several hours I bowed, greeted, hugged, and listened to many grieving neighbors and businessmen. O'Riley stood beside me, introducing me to the people with whom I was unfamiliar.

"My lady, this is Lord Cooper, First Lieutenant of Ireland." O'Riley's fluctuated tone surprised me. I glanced up at him and noticed his odd behavior. His mouth opened slightly, and, as if he were attempting to speak but the words got stuck, seemed to become frozen. He looked at me with his head cocked and one brow raised, and then began to nod slowly. I realized at that moment that I ought to pay attention to these seemingly important people.

I held up my hand as I had been trained.

"We are very sorry for your loss, my lady." Lord Cooper kissed the top of my hand. He was a distinguished-looking man, probably the same age as my father, and tall, though perhaps it was his top hat that added to his height. In his hand, I noticed he carried an exotic-looking cane that boasted an ornamental piece of gold on its crown. I hadn't seen him limping so I wondered if he carried it to convey a sense of fashion.

"My lady, Lord Cooper recently purchased a country home in Donegal Town. I presume you may encounter one another at social gatherings in the future," O'Riley said.

"I see." I smiled and nodded. "And how did you know my father?"

"Ah, yes. I first became acquainted with your father at a dinner for landlords produced by the Land League Association. A favored man he was. Unfortunately, dare I say, my work in Dublin is quite extensive this year and has kept me away from Donegal Town for some time. I certainly wish I'd been able to work alongside your father longer. Nonetheless, I'm grateful for all the ways your father brought his ideas and ambition to our committee."

"Committee?" I asked.

"Aye, the Mansion House Relief Committee. You aren't familiar with our work?"

"I'm afraid not, my lord." His condescending tone made me feel like I wanted to crawl under a rock.

"What, with all the distress our country is under? Last year's harvest proved to be the worst since the Great Famine." Lord Cooper tsked. "Unfortunately, it appears those ominous signs are reappearing across the land."

"Lady Nora has been quite busy with her studies," O'Riley said. "Rather than concern her with this year's devastating famine, John Gallagher chose to keep these affairs at bay."

"Well, I'm not sure I completely agree." Lord Cooper glanced over his shoulder at a well-groomed man who looked like a younger version of himself. "My son is privy to all my business and social affairs. I hold nothing back. Isn't that right?"

The young man, whose age appeared to slightly surpass mine, nodded and opened his mouth to speak, but his father spoke first. "Although, possibly it's different with a daughter, I wouldn't know. There are certain limitations, I suppose." The way he smiled at me gave me the sensation akin to worms crawling on my skin. "Nonetheless, my lady, our committee works with charitable organizations to raise funds so that we can provide relief to tenant farmers and families in distress. Like those poor suffering folk who've had a loss of cattle or their potato crop has failed causing them extreme misery, dare I say, starvation."

"Ach! That's horrible."

"'Tis a grand shame." Lord Cooper stepped aside. "This is my son, Albert Edward Cooper."

Albert Edward's eyes dropped, just for a moment. They were blue, the kind of blue that clouds loll upon. His round face held boyish features and his skin was soft and pale, like butter after a churn. Albert Edward stepped forward and mimicked his father's display of respect by kissing my hand. Even though he looked like his father, his demeanor felt different, genuine and sincere.

"My condolences, my lady." He seemed kind.

"I appreciate that you would travel this far to pay respects."

"Indeed," the Lord stomped his cane on the ground. "I'm certain we'll meet again. I presume whoever succeeds the affairs of Kings Castle will likely pick up where your father left off. At least the committee is hopeful. In the meantime, I believe my son will be spending a fair amount of time this summer at our country estate. I have some relief work for him to do in this area. Perhaps the two of you will have an opportunity to meet again." He gave a quick, determined look to his son.

As his father began to walk away, Albert Edward gave me a tired look, the kind of heaviness that tugs at the corner of a person's eyes like a weighted anchor at sea. *Desperation.* I knew that look. I'd seen it reflected in my mirror a thousand times. Weary from the burden of having to be, to perform, and to uphold a certain standard.

I felt a tap upon my shoulder and I turned to see Angela and John, my black frock coat draped over Angela's extended arms. John picked up the coat and helped me navigate the simple task of slipping it on.

Angela bent toward me. "How are you doing? You look tired. Perhaps you should take a rest."

"Trying to hold myself together, I suppose." I forced a smile.

I took a step closer to O'Riley. "Psst," I tugged on the cuff of his shirt coat, "I think I could use a little break."

O'Riley nodded. "I think it'd be best if you lie down for a while. I'll fetch you if you're needed for anything important."

We wove through the crowded room and found some space in the corner. "Lady Nora," John put his arm around Angela, "I . . . I don't know what to say." He stared at the floor.

Feeling chilled, I rubbed my arms. "Me too, John. Me too."

Out of the corner of my eye, I noticed a frail-looking boy walking towards me. It was Thomas, our driver. I hardly recognized him; his hair and clothes were a disheveled mess, and thick, dark shadows ringed his eyes. His usually well-kept mousey brown hair now covered his forehead and wisped over his eyes.

"I could use your help sorting through the trade. It's been sitting there for days," John whispered to Angela.

She gave him a pleading look. "Now?"

"I'm all right, Angela. You should go. Besides, I'm heading to my keep in a wee bit to go lie down." I was trying to convince Angela as much as myself that I was fine, while, secretly, I wondered if that would ever be possible.

I turned toward Thomas. He extended a shaking hand and I felt my heart soften like a patty of butter on a warm summer's day. Poor Thomas was shaken.

"Thomas?"

"Yesss, my lady." His mouth opened and closed as if he'd taken an unfavorable bite.

Thomas took a step closer to me, his head down. He began to nervously pick at his fingers. Something was amiss. When he tried to speak his words stammered out. "I . . . wo-wo-would like, my lady, to share with you s-s-some important details about the night of your father's . . . " Thomas trailed off, seemingly exhausted by the labor of his tongue.

"Aye! I have many questions for you too. I'm desperate to know who is responsible for his death."

Thomas took another step closer. "I'm sorry, I don't have that answer for you. But did y-y-you know that O'Riley has arranged a m-m-meeting at the gatehouse to go over the d-d-details of the attack?"

"I wasn't aware of any meeting." I said as I wondered why O'Riley didn't tell me. "When is it?"

"Tonight. After everyone c-c-clears out." Thomas looked around the room swollen with people. "All I can tell you is that ev-ev-everything happened so quickly. There were s-s-so many of them." He shoved his hands into his pockets and began to rock back and forth. "It seemed like such a normal day. I'd driven your father to Glenties for the signing of a new tenant contract like I'd done plenty of times before."

"Oh. Who was this contract with?"

"A m-m-man by the name of Kevin McGrath. He is a middle man, you kn-kn-know, the ones who divide the land into smaller h-h-holdings and then sublease the property to local farmers. Mr. McGrath, yeah, he earns his li-li-living by leasing out rented land."

I listened intently to every word Thomas said.

From behind me, I felt someone brush up against me. I spun my head to see who was nudging me and saw it was Jack Griffith. He moved through the room with grace, almost as if he were floating. I looked down and noticed that his feet were indeed touching the ground. And there she was, our fiddle, nestled to his side, cradled by the palm of his hand. My mouth dropped in awe. Before I could make sense of anything, I watched him glide over to the fireplace, reach above the mantel and set her in the crook of her rightful place. Of course, he knew exactly where she belonged. Mr. Griffith stopped, turned his head, and locked eyes with me. A prickly sensation overcame me and every hair on my body stood on end. There was a brilliance to his age-old face like the way the sun kisses skin on a warm day. Then without another word he turned away and began to weave himself through the room unnoticed. As quickly as he came, he slipped through the front door and back into the night.

"Everything all ri-right, my lady?" Thomas questioned with a concerned look upon his face.

I'd forgotten that Thomas was still standing in front of me.

"Ach! I'm sorry," I said as I rubbed one of my eyes. "Carry on . . . "

"Perhaps it'd be b-b-best if you went and got yourself some rest. Come to the m-m-meeting later tonight. You'll receive your sh-sh-share of details, plus whatever else O'Riley has discovered." Thomas looked over his shoulder. "I came to you be-be-because I was hoping you could m-m-meet in p-p-private. I have something I'd like to sh-sh-show you. But only you!"

I scratched my head. *Huh?*

"All right, meet me tomorrow in town at the T-T-Trading Post. It would be s-s-safer that way." Thomas jittered his foot on the floor.

"Ok, I suppose. I shall be there." *What was Thomas talking about?* My mind felt as though I'd dove into a deep pool of water without the use of my arms or legs—as though I was completely aware of my surroundings, yet unable to make my way to the surface.

Thomas turned to leave and then spun back around. "May I suggest you br-br-bring some goods with you for trade? That way no one will be s-s-suspecting anything unusual."

After dusk I made my way to the gatehouse. Leo, fully decorated in his uniform, stood upright at his post outside the building. The brim of his hat cast a slight shadow over his eyes. Leo was a friend, too, I guess. Since he and John O'Doolan were pals, most likely to chum around on their days off, we naturally found ourselves at the same social gatherings or dances.

"What are you doing, kid?" Leo looked over his shoulder into the dimly lit building behind him, "I mean, my lady." He bowed. "I'm surprised to see you here."

For as long as I can remember Leo has called me kid, but only in private, of course! It'd mean death to his career otherwise. I don't know when or how it started. Perhaps it was because Leo was nearly ten years my senior, but it never really bothered me since I didn't care much for formalities anyway. Plus, I found it endearing. Despite his status as servant and mine as lady of the house, we proved that the two could still be friends at heart.

"I am surprised too. I learned about this meeting only a wee bit ago."

"O'Riley mentioned that you had already turned in for the evening. I guess we . . . I wasn't expecting to see you."

I stood on tiptoes to peer around Leo's tall frame. The compact room was filled with men of all sizes—some in uniform, while others wore plain clothing.

"What's going on in there?"

"Apparently O'Riley received a post this afternoon. It contains some information about your . . . listen, are you sure you want to sit in on the conversation?" Leo tipped his hat exposing his green eyes and looked down at me with sincerity. I appreciated his concern, but why did it feel like he was always hovering over me like he was some kind of big brother? I guess he was only being responsible to his duty.

"I really ought to stay." I felt my face flush with color. "I have too many questions I'd like answered. I don't understand, Leo . . . who would do such a thing? My Pop was a good man, wasn't he?"

Leo gently patted my arm. "Aye, he was a very good man." He slapped his hand over his heart as if he might be choking on a piece of hard candy. "All I can say is, if it wasn't for your father I would still be a poor farm boy with no hope for a future. Your Pop, well, he gave me a second chance at life. For that, I'll forever be indebted to him." The lump in Leo's throat rolled up and down as he swallowed.

All I could do was nod. As I stepped around Leo, he gripped my arm. "If it's too much to bear, give me the sign and I'll escort you out." Leo looked down at my feet, "You remember, right?"

A few years ago, during Fair Day I had accidentally gotten battered by a brood of men who were enraged over an apparent miscalculation on a trade. I became entangled in their heated debate. Luckily, Leo rescued me from the horde of people. Later, he told me that if I ever found myself in such a position again, I needed to tap my foot three times to communicate my need for assistance. But we've never executed his plan because there hasn't been a need.

I stepped over the threshold and into the stuffy room. Leo followed closely behind. Men were gathered around a large table in the center of the room discussing matters with hard-edged tones of anger. When a few men noticed my arrival, the room seemed to silence itself.

"My lady . . . ?" O'Riley gave a quick glance over my head at Leo. "What seems to be the bother?"

"Well, I've heard something about a post, and if you don't mind, I'd like to hear the news for myself."

O'Riley sauntered over to my side. "I'm not so sure you should be here." He lowered his voice, "It's likely that many of these details will be quite unpleasant and I'd hate to add to the horror you've already been exposed to."

"Thank you for your concern, O'Riley." My voice seemed to bounce off the walls. "However, I prefer to be acquainted with the details surrounding my father's death."

O'Riley gave me a drawn out stare before he responded, "As you wish, my lady."

My insides tightened as I braced myself for the news. Standing among all these men, I needed to be strong. This was no time to show any sign of weakness.

From the corner of the room, I heard a shuffle behind several tall men. Thomas poked his small head through an opening and slipped out from behind them.

"As you may already kn-kn-know, my lady, I was present for all the events," Thomas stuttered.

"Yes, Thomas, I'm aware. I am eager to hear your account of things." I looked at him squarely, trying to avoid any suspicion that we held any secrets.

Thomas took a deep breath and resumed, "I am so very s-s-sorry for your loss. It pains me to t-t-tell you these things." His voice cracked.

"I think," O'Riley stepped in front of Thomas, "I might be able to communicate the event a bit more clearly. You don't mind, do you Thomas?"

Thomas took a step backward and his body appeared to shrink. He gave a slight nod to O'Riley as if obligated by the rank of superiority to agree.

"You see, after the business affair with the McGrath family concluded, Thomas began the regular journey home. Around dusk they approached a bend in the road and noticed a leveled field wall. Thomas reported that an entire clan of men jumped onto the path. Within a moment's notice, their lit torches encircled the jaunting car, and they began shouting in Irish. All he could make out between the clamoring was bits and pieces of their request. The word *airgead* was repeated over and over."

"They were looking for money?" I questioned.

Thomas rocked onto his toes. His eyes bounced back and forth between O'Riley and myself. "I . . . I don't remember. I mean, I . . . I don't know. But then Snow got spooked by the commotion and she r-reared up. The car then lurched and smashed onto its side. I let go of the r-reigns and watched as Snow disappeared."

Oh. So, that's how Snow cut the side of her face. A chill whipped through the room and my chin began to quiver.

"My leg was t-t-trapped beneath the wheel when the clan closed in around us. I didn't know wh-wh-what to do. They were ransacking the cart. It felt as though they had a mission, in s-s-search of something. And then, after what felt like an hour had passed, they disappeared."

"Did they discover any airgead? Was money taken?" I folded my hands behind my back to control my shaking hands.

O'Riley coughed. "I think the post we've received offers the best lead." He pulled the letter from his pocket, unfolded the piece of parchment, and began reading:

To the dearest survivors of Mr. John Gallagher,

Our condolences on your recent loss. This information is purely up for subjection; however, on the basis with which the incident has been reported, we, those of us central to the work of the Mansion House Relief, have concluded the possibility that this horrific attack may, in part, be due to the fact that Mr. John Gallagher had communicated to the committee his intent to solicit monies from Mr. Kevin McGrath, a profitable middle man, for the benefit of our relief efforts. If this is the case, we presume a sizable donation may have been confiscated. You may find it of interest to look into the matter to determine if criminals stole such benevolent monies, as we suspect. If we can be of any assistance, please let us know.

Signed,

Sir John Barrington, lord mayor of Dublin

On behalf of the Mansion House Relief Committee

That sensation of swimming underwater began to overpower me again, and it took everything I could muster to tap my foot three times.

CHAPTER 4

GETTING OUT OF BED FELT impossible. My body was weak. My chest felt as if it was being crushed beneath a boulder loosed from the sea's cliff. Wouldn't it be easier to sleep away the misery? I'd thought about playing my fiddle, but the grief seemed to swallow me too whole. Besides, I'd promised Thomas I would meet him at the Trading Post today. If it weren't for my curiosity to discover what secret he held, I'd prefer to stay beneath my coverlet.

I sat up and stared out my window. A bleak wind was bullying the trees that lined the woods edging the castle, like the grief that tormented my state of mind. I slowly climbed out of bed to dress for the day. I'd told Miss Celia the night before that I could manage the morning routine on my own. Surprisingly, she agreed. Although, not without a brief lecture on rest and the importance of taking care of myself. Fumbling through my wardrobe, I chose a plain black tailor-made suit. The wool skirt was flat in the front and flared at the back for easy walking. My arms felt heavy as I attempted to fasten the small buttons lining the bodice of my fitted suit coat. After tucking a few loose strands of hair into my boater hat, I regarded my dim reflection and sighed. *Good enough to get me through the day. If only I can manage to make it through the day.*

I trudged into the courtyard and noticed Frank awaiting me.

"Good day, my lady." He turned to finish securing the lead rope to Snow. She appeared to have some kind of ointment slathered on the side of her face over her cut.

"How is she doing?" I approached slowly.

"Very well, considering. Ya, she's bouncing back. I'm not surprised. Horses are quite resilient. The boys have ridden her several times since . . . uh, the incident. Her tongue isn't hanging out and she appears to be behaving like her normal self."

I caressed her forehead. "Her injury appears to be healing quite nicely too."

"Indeed . . ." Frank paused. His cheeks puckered as if he were chewing on his words.

"What is it, Frank?"

"I've a request. I've gone to O'Riley but he keeps putting me off. He's been mighty busy after all and I know we've all been through a lot recently. It's only . . . I'm wondering if ya might be able to help me. Ya see, Fair Day is next week and . . . "

Fair Day. The single day each month Donegal Town's Diamond transformed into a thriving marketplace. It was also the same day my Pop established our Fair Day program as a way to help families in need by giving away livestock animals like cows and chickens. It was a boost for the family, and I believe it made my father feel good too.

"Do you need help selecting which animals will be given away?"

"No. O'Riley has managed to control which stock will be doled out. Apparently we're cutting back on our donation."

"Cutting back?"

"Ya, he said I'm allowed to purchase only one animal. I'm not sure why. But my problem is that typically your father approved the recipients. There are so many to choose from, my lady. The requests for help keep comin' in. Seeing as though we're giving only a single Moiled cow this month, only one family can be awarded. I suppose I'm wonderin' what your thoughts are on choosing this month's family?"

"Oh, I see." My heart fluttered in anticipation. "Um, I don't know?" I scratched my head. "Do you know how my Pop would go about choosing?" I hoped Frank knew more than me.

"I'm sorry, my lady. I suppose O'Riley would be privy to this information. Perhaps, I've crossed a line by asking ya to choose. It's . . . well, it seems appropriate to consider your wishes."

I nodded, grateful for Frank's gesture. "I will take the liberty to discuss the matter with O'Riley and will inform you of our, ahhem . . . my decision."

"Very well." Frank smiled wearily. "Here are the items for trade ya requested. Four pounds of apples and two fox pelts." He patted the satchel harnessed to Snow's saddle. "John left them for ya, said you'd be needing them today." A look of curiosity streaked across his raised brow.

"Thank you, Frank," I said. "You have been a great help to me this morning."

As he turned away toward the stable I noticed the way his shoulders sagged. I sensed he was worried about the future of Kings Castle. Frank O'Sheen wasn't the only one.

Snow and I cantered toward the castle gate and Leo, who'd been on guard, stood at attention.

"Good day. Life opens bright, aye?"

Leo's poetic reference to Samuel Lover caused my cheeks to pinch. Leo wasn't educated in the way of famous composers but he knew full well my affection for Samuel Lover. *Morning, sweet morning, I welcome thy ray, Life opens bright like the op'ning of day.* I'd found it a lovely tune, until late. Life did not feel particularly bright these days, but I appreciated Leo's effort to elicit a smile. It worked.

"Shall you be waiting for Miss Celia to escort you?"

"Nae." I looked over my shoulder toward Miss Celia's cottage, still dark. She must be taking the opportunity I'd given her to catch up on rest. "I . . . em . . . I'll be venturing to town by myself today, thank you."

Leo's brow contracted. "With all due respect, kid. I don't quite feel right about letting you go unattended."

Suddenly, my wool suit began to itch in unreachable places. "Well." I contemplated my options, remembering Thomas' note of privacy. "I'm going. Alone. 'Tis only into town for a wee bit, Leo. Every thing will be fine, you'll see." I attempted to scratch the fiery irritation under my sleeve. "Now, if you'll kindly lift the gate."

Leo turned and began to jerk on the pulley with his ridged hands. His stiff posture and corded neck projected his response.

As I left, I began to clip down the steep cobbled pathway towards town. Our castle—our home on a hill—overlooked Donegal Town's thriving town center. Along the left side, the woods lined the edge of the path. I peered deep into the trees with wonder as the stories I'd been told since I was a wee child began to unfold in my mind. In particular, a story about a secret passageway, a tunnel through the woods that led straight into our castle cellar, surfaced. The story indicated that it'd been constructed by the Franciscan monks hundreds of years ago as an alternative escape route in case of a castle attack.

I didn't care much for that tale, and Miss Celia urged me to pay no mind to it. So, I guess, for fear of whatever might be lurking, I've always avoided exploring through the woods. And quite honestly, for that reason, that's why I kept myself from venturing to the cellar. The thought made me shiver. I looked the other way, glancing over at the rolling emerald hill along the right side of the trail. Engraved stones dotted the lush landscape marking Milmount Cemetery. It was odd to think that Pop was never coming home. That feeling of longing tingled beneath my chest. I was still numb from everything that had occurred in the last few days. I thought about Frank's inquiry surrounding Fair Day and it dawned upon me that many matters would soon fall into my care. I had watched my Pop over the years grasp all the affairs of our castle and community with unflinching confidence. *Could I really handle Kings Castle on my own?*

As I continued to the bottom of the hillside, I observed the hustle and bustle of our tidy town nestled between the groove of two mountainous valleys. From my position I could see clear across the land towards the Bluestack Mountains on the eastern horizon. The plotted land was lined with fieldstone, and seedlings from the springtime plants would be emerging soon. I found it strange*: how quickly life goes on,* I thought.

I crossed the old bridge and remembered the days Pop would take me fishing down by the river. Around this time of year, we would fish for the spring salmon. Occasionally, we would catch sea trout. The lovely thing about trout is their laziness. On a good day, if I kept my calm, I might be able to catch one with my bare hands.

I bounced past the shops, including Agee's Tweed and Fashion Shop and the Abbey Hotel, which faced each other across the street.

The Trading Post was situated on the corner at the far end of town. Sam Connor, the Trading Post master, leaned against the plastered wall with his burly arms folded across his chest and a scowl upon his round face. If I didn't know better I might chase off in the other direction because this man looked like an angry dog ready to bite. But Sam was a gentle, fair soul. He didn't have a mean bone in his body. My father had respected Sam Connor. Not only was he trusted to be fair in his dealings with trades of all kinds, Sam was also Donegal Town's official weight master on Fair Day. I'd once overheard Pop discussing with vigor the enormous responsibility a weight master had. If cantmen and dealers discovered that a town's official had cheated them in a fair wage because they'd tipped the scales, it could mean ruin for an entire town. That time I accidentally got trampled by a brood of angry men was the fault of a weight master, and so after that, Pop saw to it that the position be forever held by a man of strong character.

"Lady Nora!" Sam waved me over to the hitching post he'd been leaning against. "Let me help you with these things," he said in a low voice as he quickly began unstrapping the satchel from Snow. "Thomas mentioned you were bringing a few items for trade this morning."

"He did? I mean, yes." I did my best to speak casually. "John was uh . . . busy and ya know I thought it'd be a good way for me to pass some time." I didn't know what to say. I wasn't fibbing, exactly. John was busy. Then again, I suppose he was always busy. If this was supposed to be a secret, I wondered how Thomas would skirt around a private conversation.

"Thomas is waiting for you in the supply room. He said he'd like to have a word with you." Sam offered his hand to help me dismount.

"Come, follow me." Sam motioned, leading me down the boardwalk where two separate doors led into the Trading Post. One was located in the front of the building and was the public entrance to the mercantile, while the other door was toward the backside near the shipping dock along the river. This was a private entrance to the supply room containing traded goods stacked on shelves and placed in barrels. Many items brought in by smaller ships would be stored here until being inspected. Sam opened the door for me and I slipped inside.

"Here she is, Thomas. I'll take these few trade items up front for immediate review and record the sale."

"Th-th-thank you, Ssssam."

When Sam left, I turned towards Thomas.

"Thomas, you have done a fine job of working up a girl's suspicions. As you might imagine, my heart is in a terrible state. I hope you can explain what all this secrecy is about."

"I'm s-s-sorry, my lady. I didn't mean to . . . " Thomas handed me a tattered looking portfolio covered in dirt. "Here."

I held it momentarily before slowly turning it around in my hand. It looked familiar to me and then the smell struck me. Bay Rum, Pop's favorite cologne.

"Is this my Pop's legal portfolio?" I looked at Thomas with wide eyes.

As I carefully opened the cracked leather case, a postmarked envelope slipped into my hand. I stared at the inky words until my eyes grew dry. It was addressed to the Herbert School of Music and it appeared to be written in my father's handwriting.

"I don't understand. Where did you find this?"

"Mr. Gallagher . . . em, yer Pop handed it to me m-m-moments after . . . " Thomas flipped his head to the side, parting his hair so

I could plainly see the look of determination in his eyes. “He said, ‘Give this to Nora and tell her she will always be the Sunshine of my Heart.’”

“Ach! Speak plainly to me Thomas for I do not understand!”

“After those b-b-bandits disappeared and I was able to l-l-loose myself from beneath the wheel, I ran back to check on your f-f-father. He was not in a g-g-good way. I promised to run for help, but f-f-first, he gave me this, for you.” Thomas pressed both of his hands to the top of his head. “I still can’t believe h-h-he didn’t make it.”

I unsealed the envelope, pulled out the folded piece of parchment, and began reading the scripted letter.

> To the administrator of the Herbert School of Music;
>
> I’m writing to request admission for my daughter, Honora Katherine Gallagher, to your school of music this fall . . .

Tears began to sting my eyes. I couldn’t believe it. I quickly folded the paper and placed it back within the envelope so as not to smear the writing. Pop was really going to allow me to pursue my dream after all!

“I’m curious, did you share any of this information with O’Riley?” I felt my mouth pucker as I bit the inside of my cheek.

“No. I w-w-wanted to honor Mr. Gallagher first. I’m going to g-g-give the portfolio to the garda later today and explain that I’d picked it up in the confusion.” Thomas lowered his voice. “And one more thing . . . it’s the money. It’s missing.”

“Are you referring to the money for the Mansion House Relief Committee?”

"Yesss." Thomas nodded. "The benefit money to fund the relief efforts, as well as the rent collection dues from Mr. Kevin McGrath. All of it was s-s-stolen by those rotten scoundrels."

I shook my head. "I . . . I don't know what to do." It was true. I really didn't know how to handle such a crime. This was a job for O'Riley. I looked down and realized I had a white-knuckled grip on the letter.

"Don't w-w-worry about the money, my lady. I'm going to tell O'Riley that indeed all the money has been stolen, as s-s-suspected." Thomas pointed to the envelope in my hand. "I hope it means s-s-something to you."

"It most certainly does. How can I ever repay you!" I shook Thomas's hand.

As I rounded the corner of the Trading Post, I ran straight into a woman, knocking her petite body into the arms of the man standing next to her. She let out a muffled squeal.

"Ach, my, I'm so very sorry . . . " *Violet? And Leo?*

Violet Ellison. The pretentious daughter of David and Shannon Ellison, owners of the popular Abbey Hotel. I watched Leo help Violet straighten onto her own two feet before they both turned to look at me.

"Leo? What are you doing . . . ?" I was surprised to see him here. Was he following me? Nae. Clearly, by the way the two of them appeared to be conversing, it'd been arranged.

"Don't you bother slowing down before tearing around street corners?" Violet huffed, sweeping her skirt for composure.

"I'm terribly sorry, Violet." My hands clenched and I felt the envelope crinkle in my hand.

"I'm only kidding." Violet laughed in her signature note—a high pitch—that hurt the ears. The townsmen found it flirtatious, which many enjoyed, but it was annoying to me. I suppose Leo rather enjoyed it, though, since he'd favored Violet Ellison for as long as I could remember. Even though she'd refused his hand in marriage, I could still see the twinkle in Leo's eyes when he looked at her. I didn't see it. Sure, she was beautiful, with sleek bouncing curls the color of golden honey. But, I'd seen the way she talked about others. The way she treated people was rude. And I knew that deep down, she was not kidding. I'd always been kind to Violet, but she never seemed to reciprocate my gesture. It seemed the only interchange she enjoyed was gossiping about others.

"Sorry to bother you. Good day." I stepped around the two of them and began walking towards Snow.

"As I was saying . . . " Violet began babbling loud enough for anyone in earshot to hear, "apparently Kevin McGrath rented a parcel of land to this family and . . . "

"Excuse me, Violet." Leo interrupted her blathering. "My lady—"

I paused, turning to give Leo a curious look. The usage of my proper title coming from the lips of Leo O'Donnell reminded me that we were indeed in public.

"Are you in need of my assistance?" he said.

I shook my head, "Nae." I fumbled to unhitch Snow from her post. "I can manage."

I rode Snow back to the castle like I was escaping a vicious viper.

A knock at my door startled my thoughts. I scooped up the letter I'd been staring at on top of my desk and carefully tucked it into the center drawer.

"Come in."

Miss Celia stepped into the frame of the door.

"Leo O'Donnell has requested your presence in the great room."

"What does he want from me?"

"Honora!" Miss Celia straightened her back, "his duty is to protect and serve this castle. I'm sure the matter he wishes to discuss is important."

I took a deep breath. "Very well, then."

When I stood up, Miss Celia retreated down the hall.

In the great room, Leo was staring at a painting of my Pop and me that hung on the wall.

"If I didn't know better, I'd get off to thinking you rather enjoy following me around."

Leo turned around. "Oh yeah?" He let out an unusual laugh that stopped abruptly. "I'd like to think you *do* know me better. Following you around? I'm only doing my duty." Leo tugged the brim of his uniformed hat.

"I didn't get a chance to speak with you at the Trading Post, which is why I'd come down there to begin. But you and Snow sped off so fast, I was afraid you'd set the castle forest ablaze. Then I'd really have some explaining to do for leaving my post."

I shook my head and smiled slightly at that. "As you can see, I'm fine. No fire to report either."

"Very well." Leo took a step closer to me. His dimpled smile erased as he straightened his jacket. "I felt I should pass along some information that Violet Ellison has just shared with me."

"Is it credible?"

Leo's mouth dropped. "Why, yes, I believe it's credible."

"I just know she has a tendency to fabricate things. Anyway, carry on."

"She said a man from Glenties checked into the Abbey Hotel last night. Over dinner he told the other guests about a poor local farmer whose cows disappeared in the middle of the night."

"Cows gone missing? That seems outlandish to me. I told you Miss Ellison likes to exaggerate things."

"I honestly think she's telling the truth." Leo walked over to the table and picked up a news copy of *The Examiner.* "See." He handed me the paper and I read the headline, *Glenties Farmer Says Cows Were Stolen By Bandits.*

"Why would anyone do such a thing?"

"It's been another hard year. A spoiled harvest means that folks are desperate."

"You mean, starving."

"I'm afraid so."

I scanned the news copy looking for a name. "Oh, it says here the farmer was a man by the name of Sean Kearny."

"Aye, that is correct. Violet tells me that she heard they're renters of Kevin McGrath. You know, the man your father met."

"It's an awful shame." I shook my head. It was amazing to think how one unruly act after another could create a ripple of grief as wide as the western seaboard.

"I had a thought too, if you don't mind me sayin'."

"Of course not, Leo. What is it?"

"I was thinking we could award the Sean Kearny family with a pair of cows, among the other recipients at Fair Day next week?"

That's it. The answer Frank was looking for. There was something almost redeeming about choosing the Kearny family as the recipient for Fair Day.

"Leo. I think that sounds like a grand idea!"

Leo flashed a surprised smile.

"As well, you've heard the news, aye? That O'Riley is cutting back on the program by giving only one animal to one family," I added.

Leo tilted his head to one side. "I'm afraid I wasn't aware of this change. Who told you this?"

"Frank. He said O'Riley spoke to him."

"Hmm. Don't worry, I'll investigate. I'm sure it's only temporary because of the state we've been placed under as of late."

CHAPTER 5

WHEN I WAS A KID there was one day out of the whole month when the regimen didn't get the best of me. It was Fair Day. A single day when the order of Kings Castle, with its proper *this* and proper *that,* seemed to relax and let me be a regular person. On Fair Day, farmers and their families, cantmen with their deals, and revelers without inhibitions would travel near and far to participate in the festivities. Pop never really included me in any of his business affairs, but whenever Fair Day rolled around, I was able to see him in his element. He always smiled a bit more on these days.

I stood before my window and watched the bustling courtyard below. The wooly yearling and spotted calves, just weaned from their mother's milk, were being gathered from the livery. Our team of horses, hitched to the wagon, seemed to stand tall with their chests puffed and chins held high, each reflecting the gleam of their polished bridle. Usually servants would load crates of produce and textiles onto the wagon, but today was different. The view from above showed a sparsely filled wagon. Perhaps this reminder that Pop wasn't ever coming home was the reason it felt like a millstone was tied around my heart. Leo had reported that the Kearny family would be traveling into town to receive their gift of a Moiled cow. I intended to go so that I could grant them their animal. I believe it's what Pop would have wanted, despite my feelings of desperately wishing to remain indoors away from the noise and away from well-meaning people.

When I stepped out into the courtyard, a gentle breeze swirled about and I watched a faint cyclone of dust dance across the vacant grounds. Most of the servants had already departed for town, except Frank.

"I've saddled Snow for your ride into town today." Frank pointed toward the gatehouse where Snow had been hitched next to a pair of unfamiliar horses. That was odd. *Who was visiting the castle?*

"Very well, Frank. I shall meet up with you in a wee bit." Frank nodded and turned back toward the livery. As I continued towards the gatehouse, Leo came out of the quarters, closing the door behind him.

"Nora?" his mouth dropped slightly as if he were astonished to see me. "I presumed you would be at the Diamond already. Aren't you going to assist the gift giving for the Kearny household?"

"Indeed, I'm planning to venture in that direction." I strained my neck in an attempt to see beyond the doorframe.

"Who is visiting today?" I asked.

"It's the Aiken brothers. The lawyers representing Kings Castle. O'Riley didn't inform you?"

I shook my head. "What do they want?"

"I'm not exactly sure since I was asked to leave. But your name and something about the inheritance was mentioned." Leo turned his head from side to side. "Listen, I know you're needed in town, but maybe it wouldn't hurt to inquire." Leo shrugged.

I scooted past Leo, knocked twice upon the door, and stepped inside the gatehouse. Sitting at the table were two men I had never met before. They stood abruptly when they noticed me enter the room.

"My lady, your timing is impeccable." O'Riley's voice shook. Was he nervous? O'Riley placed his hand on my back and nudged me toward the table. "I'd like you to meet Lawrence Aiken." He waved his free hand at the lanky gentleman on the left elaborately dressed in a lounge-style suit jacket with silk braided trimmings, waistcoat, and necktie.

"Nice to meet you." I curtseyed.

"And his brother Steven Aiken." O'Riley shifted his attention to the other man who, although dressed in similar fashion, was shorter than his brother. "They've arrived from their law office in Lifford. These fine men have provided legal counsel to your Pop for as long as I can remember."

Steven saluted me by removing his top hat, exposing a more extreme difference in height than I'd previously examined. His thin hair was combed over the top of his balding head, and when he smiled, his cheeks formed a bright circle like a cherry tart.

"It's very nice to finally meet you, Honora Gallagher. Your father was a long time client and we will sorely miss him."

"They have arrived to announce the estate matters at hand," O'Riley said.

Lawrence stood tall, his top hat adding to his measure. There was an air of sophistication about him.

"I wish our meeting one another was under different circumstances." Lawrence sighed and it gave me a weird feeling.

"I agree." I swallowed the bubble of regret that caught up in my chest.

"You should know that we halted our other business affairs and promptly began traveling as soon as we heard the news," Lawrence said.

His words gave me the impression that my father's death was a thorn in his side. "Eh, I'm sorry to inconvenience you then? I'm sure this could have waited until . . . "

"Actually, no. This matter, the terms in which your father has set forth, is rather urgent."

"Oh." I didn't know what to say. I looked down at the table where they were sitting and noticed a sea of papers strewn about.

"You do understand why we have come, my lady?" Steven asked.

I opened my mouth, but before I could speak Lawrence spouted, "We are here to discuss the ownership and entitlement of Kings Castle." He turned his back to me and began shuffling some papers on the table.

"If you'll pardon my brother," Steven said. "I believe what Lawrence is trying to say is that our firm holds the will your father established in the event of his unfortunate passing." Steven's soft-spoken words helped to calm my rapidly beating heart. "It spells out the conditions which determine who shall become the rightful heir to the castle."

Ever since Pop died, I never once thought about the legal matters. I suppose I thought about the decisions that would need to be made and assumed I would be allowed to have input, but an heir? On one hand, it never occurred to me that anyone else would take over the affairs of the castle. I had no siblings. Mam was gone. All of Pop's family had either immigrated to America or passed on. And this was my home—the only home I'd ever known. It seemed only natural and right that I would be left to care for the castle. And yet, it all seemed so unnatural. In recent days, I'd contemplated if I could really take on such a monumental task. Besides, what about my dream of attending the Herbert School of Music? Especially now that I knew for certain Pop was going to bless my pursuit.

"What do you need from me?" I cleared my throat. "A signature perhaps?" It was the first idea that came to mind.

"My lady, Honora, the will and trust are a complicated matter," Lawrence said. The corner of his mouth turned slightly. "It requires more than adding your signature to a line. First, you must clearly understand the terms set forth."

I felt a flush of embarrassment.

"Listen," Steven spoke, "I know all of this is probably confusing, but our job is to carry out your father's wishes. I'm sure you want this too."

I nodded in agreement.

"Very well, we can begin by reviewing the documents and answering any questions you may have."

Just then, the door flung open and a large gust of wind came rushing in. The papers on the table began blowing around the room like scattered dandelion seeds. O'Riley rushed to save a handful of flitting papers swooping towards the burning fireplace, while Steven collapsed to his knees in an effort to collect the documents strewn across the floor. Lawrence strode across the room and slammed the door shut. His hat nearly tipped off his head exposing a few strands of tousled hair. I watched as they began sorting through the pages, laying them out on the table to get everything back into order. As I looked around the room I noticed some extra papers had drifted toward O'Riley's desk in the corner of the room.

As I proceeded to collect them, a black binder on the edge of his workspace caught my attention. It was thick and leather bound. What was it? I looked over my shoulder. The men were busy piecing the various documents back together as if they were putting together a puzzle. I couldn't tame my curiosity so I lifted the cover and peeked underneath. Several straight, lined columns showed some sort of mathematic problem solving. At the top of the page it read, *Financial Ledger.*

Oh, apparently this was the record of the castle's financial comings and goings. Looking at all those numbers made my head spin. I had no idea it required so much effort to manage the castle. I closed the cover and stooped down to pick up the scattered papers.

"Here are a few more." I walked over and placed them on the table. "Were you able to find all the documents?"

"Aye," Steven said. "I think we have everything. If you'll kindly take a seat, we weren't expecting you so we need a few minutes to get everything in order. Then we can explain what your inheritance looks like."

My inheritance? The word in itself seemed absurd.

When they were ready, Lawrence pushed a thick stack of papers across the table for me and O'Riley, who'd taken a seat next to me, to review.

LAST WILL & TESTAMENT

Herein for John Patrick Gallagher on this date of February Twenty-first in the year of Eighteen Hundred & Eighty . . .

Immediately, I noticed the date listed on the title. *Only a few months ago?* I flipped over the top page of the document and began reading, quickly overcome with legal nonsense.

"Honora, do you understand the details written in your father's Last Will and Testament?" Lawrence pointedly asked.

"I'll be honest with you Mr. Aiken, this is not an area I'm accustomed to. My father took great care of this estate, but unfortunately did not take the liberty to concern me with such legal matters. Would you be so kind as to explain?"

"Why yes, this is precisely why we are here." Lawrence puffed out his chest.

"My lady," Steven's words were gentle. "Perhaps I could outline your inheritance for you. Then, should you have any questions, we can further discuss them. Does this suit you?"

I nodded and felt a little more relaxed with Steven taking the lead.

"You've stated your lack of knowledge in legal matters. Pardon, but may I assume you are unfamiliar with the law of primogeniture?"

I shrugged. "That is correct. I don't believe I've ever heard of it."

"Okay. Primogeniture is the practice in which, upon the death of parents, the firstborn male inherits the estate."

"Oh. But there is no firstborn male or any male sibling for that matter."

Lawrence piped in, "Aye, that is correct." He then looked at his brother and chuckled. "The girl is smarter than we thought."

Steven ignored his brother's rude comment. "Honora, do you mind reading aloud the portion titled *Part I* on the page before you?" Steven asked.

"Indeed," I said looking down at the page.

"I appoint therein Honora Katherine Gallagher to administer the affairs of the estate created hereunder for Kings Castle, as defined in the said Provisions."

The Aiken brothers seemed void of expression. I turned to look at O'Riley who squirmed as if he were sitting on a cushion of needles.

"Pardon my lack of knowledge, but it appears this states I have been charged to the care of the estate."

"In essence, that is correct Honora," Steven replied.

"So, how does the law of primogeniture affect this?"

"Well, you'll find the law is overruled if the said condition is met . . . " Lawrence straightened himself and began fumbling through a few papers sitting in front of him. Pulling another document from the pile, he handed it across the table to me.

"Placed before you is the list of said *Provisions.* Be advised that your ability to retain your inheritance hinges on one specific item. If you are unable to adhere to this arrangement, your good fortune will be acquitted. Do you understand?"

I ignored Lawrence's condescending question and read the bold statement:

> The named Trustee, Honora Katherine Gallagher, must enter into the sacred bonds of marriage within one year of the said commencement. Failure to do so will result in the implementation of a secondary trustee and the rightful inheritance shall be forfeited.

"I'm required to get married?" This did not make sense to me.

"You are correct. And you have precisely twelve months to do so." Lawrence clapped his hands together. "Certainly, it's rare for a woman to inherit land or property these days, but John Gallagher was determined to ensure that Kings Castle be afforded the chance to remain with his one and only daughter, so long as you wed."

Red O'Riley sat straight as a board in his chair. "And what about the commencement?"

"Yes. Thank you for asking, O'Riley." Lawrence grinned. "We've determined to make an announcement in the Diamond during today's Fair Day gathering."

"That is, my lady, if you'll consent," Steven remarked.

"What do you mean by announcement?" My head began to pound.

"The commencement of the will includes a proper announcement to the general public. Don't worry, you need not be present, my lady. 'Tis a simple legal formality."

The lines on the paper began to blur into a fuzzy mess. I shook my head as I felt a small ember beneath my rib cage begin to lap its way up my chest.

"Tell me, what if I do not wed within the specified timeframe?" I whispered. "Then . . . then, what happens?"

Lawrence smirked in a way that led me to believe he savored this sort of knowledge. He leaned forward, scrolled his finger down the document, and began tapping the line titled *Temporary Trustee.*

> Should Honora Katherine Gallagher therefore be unable to find a suitor in marriage within the subsequent 12 months, the Temporary Trustee shall be granted to the eldest, living male relative, Mr. Tremore Gallagher of Waterford.

My mind scrambled to consider this oldest male relative. Tremore Gallagher? I recalled a distant cousin visiting the castle when I was a wee girl . . . *was it him? Would he become the Temporary Trustee?*

"Do you remember your cousin, Tremore?" O'Riley pierced me with a squinted look. It was as if he wanted me to labor upon discovering my memory of this relative.

"Not really."

"Ah, I suppose, 'tis a number of years that have passed." O'Riley scratched his head. "You would have seen him at your Grandmam's funeral when we traveled to Waterford. And I believe the last time he visited was while his father, your Uncle Donahue, was still alive. Then again, you were still a wee one when all this transpired."

"How can this be?" I asked. "I just don't understand this Provision."

"It's a measure established to protect the castle from ruin. The condition to wed is an incentive to make sure that you'll be properly cared for," Steven remarked.

Properly cared for? What? I didn't see the need to require that I wed. Wasn't our castle in good standing? Surely, I could learn to manage the affairs on my own.

Donegal Town flourished with activity as everyone rode through the main street, headed towards the Diamond. A dusty haze lingered in the air from the chaos of wagons and shuffling feet. Kings Castle servants had erected a tent for the day. As I found it and stepped inside the empty tent, I noticed Frank on his knees sorting a few items of produce when I approached.

"My lady, ya missed the Kearny family."

"Ach! I'm sorry. I got caught up in something at the castle. That's disappointing; I really wanted to meet them."

"Ya, they took their calf and began their journey home. They asked that I extend their deep gratitude to the castle for such a gift." Frank looked across the open square towards the growing mass of people.

Curious about what captivated Frank's attention, I turned around and watched Sam Connor carefully wheel the scales from behind Agee's Tweed and Fashion Shop towards the iron triangle, a platform secured to the center of the Diamond. After pushing the heavy scales, Sam scooped them up with one flexed arm and hung them from the iron triangle.

"Who are those men standing with O'Riley?" Frank asked as he pointed toward the center of the large crowd.

The Aiken brothers had prominently positioned themselves in the heart of town. This being the busiest of market days, travelers from near and far would soon be privy to the condition of my inheritance.

"Pop's attorneys," I mumbled. "They've arrived to ruin what remains of my now-miserable life." Once the harsh words spilled out of my mouth, I regretted them. How could I say such a horrible thing? I couldn't help the feelings of total abandonment.

I began walking towards the crowded square as if I were a prisoner walking the plank to her doom. The smell of roasted pork co-mingled with unwashed travelers was making me nauseous. Or maybe it was the notion that my name would soon be the topic of every conversation. I looked around at the various dealers and noticed Jack Griffith set up in his usual position, on the corner. A humble array of pots and wares for sale were displayed on wooden crates.

As I approached the Aiken brothers, the crowds began to part like the Red Sea. Women began whispering and pointing. Men bowed before me, a gesture I was required to acknowledge. Suddenly, there was a bright flash and a *pop* boomed in my ear. The photographer from *The Examiner* was drawing even more attention to me! I felt as if I were in a dream: wishing I could run fast and far away, but powerless to do so.

I stood fastened to O'Riley's side as the Aiken brothers publicly declared my future before the crowd.

CHAPTER 6

OUTSIDE OF THE LIVERY, THOMAS was repairing the wooden wheel to the jaunting car when I stopped to greet him.

He reported to me that Miss Celia didn't seem her usual self and perhaps I should consider paying a visit. I'd had very little interaction with her over the past couple days, so I decided that might be a good idea; however, I wasn't looking forward to the questions I imagined awaited me. I made a brief visit to Miss Pavek to gather a small basket of bread and jam for Miss Celia. As I stood in front of Miss Celia's stone cottage door, I tucked a few loose strands of hair beneath my hat and straightened my blouse before knocking.

"What can I do for you, my lady?" Miss Celia said opening the door and then leaning against the door as though it were a crutch. I noted, as Thomas suggested, her state to be unusually subdued.

"Oh." *Why did I stop again?* I turned my head and saw that across the courtyard O'Riley was speaking with Thomas. "Um, I thought you might enjoy a treat from Miss Pavek." I handed her the basket. As Miss Celia accepted the basket, she invited me inside. When I stepped into her home, the somber air felt as though it were constricting my skin.

"Take a seat." Miss Celia motioned with her hand towards the square table in the center of her single-room home. In one corner was her neatly arranged bed and on the opposite end, a rocking chair sat next to the fireplace.

"Can I pour you some tea?" she inquired, hunching over a humble stack of peat logs. Miss Celia took one and placed it on the dwindling fire.

"That would be grand." I glanced around, admiring her tidy and well-kept home. Miss Celia did have a fine way of keeping order. I suppose living alone all these years had allowed her more time to fuss over the little things. On the table I noticed a wooden box filled with a stack of letters addressed to me. *What? Why was my name addressed on each envelope?*

"What in the world is this about?" I said pulling a few envelopes from the box.

"They are your requests," Miss Celia said as she set two mugs of steaming tea on the table. Then she slouched in the seat across from me.

"Requests? What do you mean?"

"Now that the condition for your inheritance has been made public, you can expect to be quite sought after. Most likely, you'll discover these letters will include invitations to a host of events such as dinner parties or charity events. It's all part of the process to vie for your hand." Miss Celia began to cough.

"Are you feeling all right?"

"Who, me? I'm fine. Probably just a little cold. I've heard one is making the rounds."

"Oh." I returned my attention to the pile of letters. *How could this be?* The thought of entertaining each request filled me with dread. As I thumbed through the pile, only one familiar name stuck out to me,

Albert Edward Cooper. I paused to remember my brief encounter with him after Pop's funeral. He seemed like a kind and decent man. I set aside the remaining letters but opened Albert Edward's. He was complimentary of our meeting and wondered if I might find interest in going riding when he returned to Donegal Town on holiday. His simple invitation caused me to reconsider my initial thoughts of agony.

"May I offer a suggestion?" Miss Celia asked.

That was odd. Miss Celia asking for my permission to receive her advice? This was new. Surely, she was coming down with sickness.

"Of course, you may."

"I understand that you are probably feeling very overwhelmed at present. Maybe even confused. Right now, the thought of finding a suitor appears to be a daunting task, one that's irrelevant and unimportant. Yet, it's fair to acknowledge that this is what your father would have wanted. My suggestion is that you open your heart and mind to the possibility of love."

I took a sip of tea to relieve my dry throat. "What if this isn't what I'd hoped for? Not now, anyway. Sure, some day I'd like to discover love and get married."

"These unexpected tragedies change us. It's hard to accept change when it's not what you've wanted nor desired for your life. But the good Lord is always faithful."

There it was, the preaching of God's faithfulness.

"I don't think I'll ever see it that way."

"What I mean is that no matter the pain we must go through, no matter the things that don't go our way, God is always working something out for good. Although you can't see it, He's been preparing you for this moment your whole life."

"What about my dream to play my fiddle . . . " I felt a cool sensation creep across my skin like the way a slow moving cloud covers the warm sun.

"Yes, Honora. God knows your desires. But He also knows what is the very best for you. It's the same with your father. He knew your desire, but marriage is what he believed would be best for you. Can't you see that perhaps he established this condition as a way to protect you?" Miss Celia's voice trailed off.

"Perhaps at one time he believed that would be best. But what if he changed his mind?" For a fleeting moment I considered telling Miss Celia about the letter Thomas had given me.

"Trust me, you don't realize how hard it is to be alone," she said. Miss Celia reached across the table and gently patted my arm. "In many regards, I understand how you're feeling. Though I've tried to hold myself together, the truth is that I, too, am in a terrible state of grief." Miss Celia's lip began to quiver. Her distress caught me off guard, so both of us sat for a moment in silence, a vain attempt to gird our emotional stability.

"There are a lot of things I wish I'd told your father. Yet, I simply couldn't find the courage, and now 'tis too late. He is gone and I fear I will live out the rest of my days in regret, remorseful that I never told him how I truly felt." A tear streaked Miss Celia's cheek.

I felt my eyes narrow. What was Miss Celia referring to? I mean, I too felt the pain of words left unsaid. For instance, why didn't Pop inform me that he approved of the Herbert School of Music? Sure, I had the letter to cling to and yet, so many unanswered questions lingered. *But what was Miss Celia talking about?*

"What sort of things?"

Miss Celia picked at the handle of her mug. "I wish I'd told your father how grateful I was—am—for his saving me."

"Saving you?"

"Aye, as you know, I grew up in town by the fisher's market. 'Twas a shack made of mud and thatch that we lived in. My Da was a hard-working fisherman, but without any land to claim his own, we were poor. One day when I was a much younger lady, yer Pop came down to the market lookin' for a few good men to help with a restoration project on the castle. My Da was hired for the job and for the first time I can remember, we didn't have to struggle to put a wee bit of food on the table."

The color from Miss Celia's face drained as she continued.

"After the work was finished, my Da fell ill and passed away. I was only sixteen, and much like you, had to learn about loss and living without my Da. It was hard. My Mam attempted odd jobs here and there, but she was never able to make ends meet. I had to do something so I decided to quit school and go out and find myself more work. I prayed that God would lead me to a decent job. That very day, as I was walking through town, I stopped off at the Trading Post to check the postings board for anyone looking to hire. I was so desperate and searching for any sort of work. As fate would have it, I bumped into yer Pop. He remembered me from the fisherman's dock and asked about my Da. When I explained the pitiful state our family was in due to his passing, yer Pop was moved to compassion. He offered me a job as a housemaid on the spot and I set to work. This, of course, was merely weeks before you were born. 'Tis hard to believe nearly eighteen years has come and gone." She shook her head. "I wish I'd told him how much he meant to me."

I caught a flicker in Miss Celia's eyes before she quickly turned to hide her face. What was it? A memory? Embarrassment? Guilt?

"Long ago I held a secret affection for yer Pop. Perhaps, I put him on too high a pedestal. Perhaps, there was something more . . . " Miss Celia's finger began to tremble as she tapped the side of her mug. "If you could have seen the affection he carried for yer Mam . . . it was a grand sight. I'd be remiss to say that I didn't have a slight longing for what they shared. He loved her all the same straight up until the day he died."

Miss Celia paused. An almost magical silence filled the room and it was as though her words of truth contained fragile particles of healing.

"It warms my heart to hear these stories." I took a sip of tea. "If you don't mind me asking, why, then, have you chosen to remain a spinster if marriage is what you've longed for?" It was a question I'd always wondered but never felt I could ask.

Miss Celia straightened her posture. "Because you needed me. After yer Mam died and yer Pop was in such a terrible state of grief, I became determined to focus on my duty to you. I learned to push away those deep-seeded dreams. Yer Pop needed my help in a desperate way." Miss Celia relaxed her shoulders for a moment. "Truth be told, I vowed that I would pour myself into your care and upbringing."

I couldn't believe what Miss Celia was saying. That she would sacrifice her own longings because of her duty . . . to me? It seemed inconceivable to me that she would offer her life in that manner. And to think, all along, I'd viewed her as a thorn in my side.

"How could you set your own ambitions aside? Maybe I should learn to push away my feelings. Perhaps life would be easier."

"The easy way is not always the best way." Miss Celia looked away from me and blotted the tears that continued to fall.

"What a shameful person I am to even tell you these things. I'm sorry, Honora, for my thoughtful disgrace. Perhaps I should never have shared these things with you. How could you ever forgive a person like me?" Miss Celia cried.

I felt like I wanted to hug Miss Celia. Would she find that gesture strange? She was always so strong; I've never seen her so broken down in all my life. Miss Celia took a deep breath attempting to regain her composure.

"You've nothing to be ashamed of." I reached across the table and squeezed her hand. A strange awe came over me and suddenly Miss Celia appeared different to me. She lifted her head and examined my eyes with an empathetic gaze as the color returned to her face. The lines around her eyes seemed less visible too. For the first time, I felt a softening between the two of us. It was as if seeing her weakened state evoked a level of understanding that never existed before. Miss Celia was a real woman, and like me, she'd experienced tragedy and loss. If she could survive, so could I.

"I'm sure this all sounds absurd but, I've thought long and hard about my decision to share these things with you. I even visited with Father Reed because I desired to be free from these thoughts that've held me captive for so long. It was his idea that I prayerfully consider laying before you this aching void I've held for so long. Honora, I do not wish to add onto yer burdens for I know they are great. But I can see that you are blossoming into a beautiful woman and I want you to know that my commitment to you will not waver. This time however, I want to do things the right way by honoring God first and foremost."

Miss Celia's words were like the sweet substance of honey. For the first time in our relationship, I felt connected.

"My dear Miss Celia," I spoke directly, "I remember someone once taught me that when you ask God for forgiveness, that it is finished. We are free." Miss Celia lifted her chin, a realization that her instruction was coming full circle. "I don't want you to live this life full of regret."

The very words, as they escaped from my lungs, caused me to sit up straight in my chair and I watched the hair on my arms rise. *Life, full of regret.*

The change in my expression did not go unnoticed by Miss Celia. "What seems to be the bother?"

My chest felt tight as I contemplated sharing the discovery of Pop's letter to the Herbert School of Music. I gasped, realizing I'd been holding my breath.

"I believe it is my turn to confide in you. Perhaps you can assist me in sorting out my feelings."

Miss Celia tilted her head, giving me a perplexed look.

"There was a letter written by Pop on my behalf. Thomas was given . . . um . . . discovered it at the scene of the incident. I've just recently been made aware of it and I think it changes things in a big way."

"What did it say?" Miss Celia leaned forward.

"The letter was written to the Herbert School of Music requesting my admittance this coming year. It had even been postmarked, ready for delivery. Understand, every time I'd expressed my desire with Pop, he always brushed me off saying he'd consider it, yet nothing ever came about, so this discovery changes everything. Don't you agree? Especially now as the measures to receive the inheritance of Kings Castle have been so clearly spelled out. How can I go about leaving the castle behind at a time such as this? And yet, knowing that Pop was going to honor my wish to pursue music, I can't help but think . . . "

"Think about what?"

"If I should forego music school to honor—"

My sentence was cut off by the sound of a loud bang at the door. We both gasped as Thomas burst through the door. He doubled over; gasping to catch his breath, "Help! Help me!"

CHAPTER 7

"THOMAS?" I SAID, STARTLED BY his frantic state. He slammed the cottage door and shuffled to the edge of the window frame, taking a quick peek out into the courtyard. He then spun around and pressed his back flat against the wall as he attempted to catch his breath.

I stood up, unsure if I should reach out to him. "What in the world is going on?"

"They're go-go-going to arrest me!"

"Who's going to arrest you?" Miss Celia interjected.

"The garda. They are a-a-accusing me of treason!"

"Treason? Whatever for?" My mind was fumbling in a hazy stupor.

"I don't know, I mean, I don't unders-s-s-stand. O'Riley's pointing his finger at me, telling the garda that I s-s-stole the monies on that fateful day. It's not true. They're even s-s-saying that I've fabricated the story!" Thomas slid his hand up the window frame, peeking his head to grab a quick view of the courtyard. "They're coming! They're coming!"

My body was stiff. I felt momentarily paralyzed until a loud banging on the door jolted my limbs back to life. Miss Celia hurried to open the door.

"Where is he?" O'Riley demanded before stepping into the room. Five garda officers immediately followed and rushed to apprehend Thomas.

As they began lugging him from the cottage I exclaimed, "Wait! Tell me what this is all about!"

O'Riley stomped towards me and in a sharp tone said, "It's quite disturbing, Honora. We've found the bandits: the same rabble-rousing group of young men who stole Mr. Kearny's cattle. They've also been heard bragging about the attack on yer Pop. In the process, we've uncovered some alarming information about our seemingly innocent driver, Thomas. This should be no bother to you, we can manage to resolve things from here on out."

"He's lying! This whole thing is a mix up! I would n-n-never betray—" Thomas shouted.

"Get that cowardly boy outta here!" O'Riley demanded. Miss Celia and I stood side-by-side in the doorway, our mouths gaping in awe, as the garda officers drug Thomas across the courtyard.

"Honora, y-y-you have to believe me! Y-y-you have to believe me! 'Tis all a mis-s-stake!" Thomas pleaded until his words trailed away and his body disappeared around the corner.

I flashed a look at Miss Celia, "Are they taking him . . . down there?"

"It appears so." *Down there: the cellar below the kitchen.* The place I dared to never venture because of its dark fable—that story I'd regretfully overheard growing up. Of course, Miss Pavek and the cooks ventured down those stone steps to acquire their root vegetables and canned goods from one of the rooms. Even the barrel of butter was kept in the cool storage room. There were other rooms too, I'd heard; one of which was where prisoners were kept while they awaited deportation. It'd been rumored that one prisoner had died down there a hundred years ago. Of course, this was long before our family took residence so I didn't know if it was true or not, but I didn't want to ever go down there and see.

"Come now, we need to trust that O'Riley has everything under control." Miss Celia pulled me away from outside and closed the door.

"Why would Thomas steal the money?" It didn't add up, especially considering Thomas had been so eager to share the letter Pop had penned to the Herbert School of Music on my behalf.

"I'm not sure, my lady. I think 'tis best that we simply allow O'Riley and the garda to handle it. I know 'tis hard to put it out of yer mind, but there are other matters that require yer attention at this time," Miss Celia said as she returned to the table, picked up the stack of invitations addressed to me, and placed them into the palm of my hand.

I was surprised to discover that Leo wasn't with the garda as they stormed Miss Celia's cottage looking for Thomas. It seemed unlike him to not be present when something big was handed down. And I know Miss Celia suggested that I let O'Riley and the others handle the issue with Thomas, but I needed clarity. I needed to find Leo. Perhaps he could give me more answers.

In the courtyard, I trailed along the pebbled walkway to the gatehouse. The sun was setting, shooting bright streaks of orange, pink, and gold across the horizon; it nearly took my breath away. Ever since Pop died, I found myself struck with awe over things I'd hardly noticed before. It was strange. But for a moment, the beauty of that sunset made me feel at peace, like Pop was surrounding me with his presence.

The gatehouse door was open a crack so I let myself in. Leo was alone, hunched over the table, and he appeared to be in deep thought by the way his brow creased in examination of what lie before him.

"You're exactly the person I was hoping to find!" I announced.

Leo jumped. "Nora? What are you doing here?"

"You know they've just arrested Thomas?"

The corners of Leo's mouth fell into a somber expression. He nodded slowly.

"This is absurd! Thomas is innocent, isn't he? Please tell me what in the world is going on. O'Riley insists that he has everything under control."

Leo picked up the piece of paper he'd been looking at and began to explain "Did O'Riley explain that several young fellas have been arrested on suspicion of your father's murder?"

"He mentioned it."

"It turns out, in their testimony they confessed to ambushing your father's jaunting car with the hope of stealing money. As we know, this collaboration proved successful, as the monies collected for rent, as well as the monies for the Mansion House Relief, have gone missing. The problem, however, is that these young fellas claim that Thomas was their co-conspirator leading them to the isolated location where they'd be able to pull off a robbery without much suspicion. Except, as we now know, things didn't go exactly as planned. And in the process your father was crushed beneath the jaunting car when it accidentally flipped over." Leo's blue eyes seemed to turn dark like a berry ripe for picking.

"You don't believe Thomas would do such a thing, do you?"

Leo folded his arms across his chest. "I've known Thomas for quite some time. I have a hard time believing he would betray your father in such a way. Sure, he's probably in need of extra money. Who isn't these days? But to plot a robbery of this significance goes against the sort of person I've known him to be."

I nodded in agreement. Something was off. If only we could get to Thomas and ask him some questions.

"Well, what do you think we should do?" No sooner did the words escape my mouth than a shiver bolted like lightning through my spine. Surely there was another way. There had to be! One of us would need to pay a visit to Thomas who was locked away in the cellar below the castle. I dared to admit it at first, but I knew that it was time to face my fear.

"You remember the plan?" Leo spoke firmly as he opened the cellar door and looked me up and down. "You'll follow the long corridor until you reach the large door on the right. It's bolted and you'll know it's the right one by the metal slates along the bottom half of the door." Leo cupped my hand into his sweating palm. "You'll need these." He wrapped my fingers around the base of a candlestick and placed a tin of matches in the palm of my other hand. "I wish I could go with you." Leo looked around the eerily-quiet kitchen.

"I wish you could too," I bit my lip, "But I need you to stay here and keep watch."

"I promise. I'll make sure no one disturbs you. We shouldn't have any problems since everyone has turned in for the night."

I stood at the top of those stairs and looked down. My heart was beating so loudly that my ears seemed to buzz, making it difficult to fully listen to everything Leo was telling me. After all these years of avoiding the cellar, was I really going to do this? That story wasn't real, I chanted to myself. I decided that I had to muster the courage so that I could uncover the truth from Thomas. Sometimes you have to face the dark to reveal truth—that was my quest.

I stepped down one crumbly step at a time. As the light faded from above, I kept my eye on the dim light projected from my meager candle. At the base of the stairs, I was forced to turn left. Right away, along the side of the corridor, I noticed an open doorway. I held up my light to see inside. It was the cellar room. Inside it was lined with shelves, most of them surprisingly bare. I saw a single basket of potatoes, a few jars of boiled meat, and a tattered sciob basket used for draining potatoes. For all these years, I'd imagined the cellar room to be stocked with an overflow of produce and goods; this famished looking room was nothing like I'd expected. I turned to keep walking forward, feeling as though I was being tugged by the black cavity ahead of me. Suddenly, I felt breathless. Stopping for a moment, I leaned against the wall to think. My eyes squeezed shut, and perspiration prickled at my neck. *I should turn back. I don't think I can do this.* Within moments, my thick hair seemed to expand under the damp conditions. *How close am I from that despised dungeon?* I wondered. My lily-livered state was causing a panic and I was beginning to regret my choice. As I focused on breathing, an image of Pop came flooding into my mind. *That's odd.* I pictured us sitting at the old pier talking, as if he were still here. *For Pop,* that's why I had to keep going. If Thomas truly was innocent, which I believed that he was, I needed to fight to defend him. I know Pop would do the same if a man were being unjustly accused.

A sickening feeling swirled in the pit of my stomach, and my vision made a sudden loop. I touched the ice-cold wall to steady my balance and felt my fingertips go numb at the touch. I shuffled my feet a few steps, with my hand outstretched before me, feeling the way. I stopped short as my fingers jammed against a chunk of iron. I wiggled my trembling hand over the knobby piece, a hinge. It was smaller than I had imagined. The thick wooden door was armored with heavy wrought iron bolts. A small metal slit the size of a platter mouthed the bottom part of the door, and chains dangled from the hefty timber log lodged across the frame of the prison door. I pulled my hand back quickly and I couldn't help but pinch my eyes closed again.

"Thomas?" I asked, my voice sounding muffled. A scuffle from behind the door made me feel like I wanted to scream.

"Who, who g-g-goes there?" Thomas stuttered.

"It's me. Lady Nora."

"My lady, y-y-you have to get me out of here!" Thomas pounded on the door. "They are accusing me of s-s-something I did not do." His adolescent voice began to whimper.

"Thomas, listen, we don't have much time. You need to tell me why O'Riley believes you would conspire to have my father robbed."

"I d-d-don't know. All I can tell you is that I never had any contact with the likes of s-s-such fools."

All at once I heard an echo of voices bouncing off the concave walls. There were deep voices speaking back and forth—I could tell at least one was Leo from the top of the stairs. And suddenly the kitchen door slammed shut, extinguishing any extra illumination to this forsaken corridor.

"Oh no! Thomas! I can't see!" I sucked for air. The confusion of voices thundered from above. Then, I heard the sound of metal scratching across metal. *The dead bolt.* "What's happening? Have I been locked in the down here?"

"Can y-y-you go pound on the door?"

I maneuvered through the dark space before me, my candle barely retaining its flame. Carefully walking up each step, I listened for the sound of that familiar voice. But there were no voices—only silence. I gripped the iron handle attempting to free myself, but it was firmly latched. As I'd suspected, it was locked. I rapped a few times and there was nothing but deafening silence. Before long, my short knocking turned into a fully unraveled pounding. Yelling turned over to screams, which eventually turned over to muffled sobs. *Would anyone let me out of this forsaken place?*

I returned to Thomas exasperated by my attempts to flee this ugly hole. "I should have never come here. What have I done? How could Leo lock the door if he knew I was down here? Worse, how could Leo abandon me? He promised."

"Wait!" Thomas hushed. "There's a-a-another way."

"Huh?"

"Yes! I d-d-don't know for certain but l-l-legend has it that a t-t-tunnel—"

"Ach! Yes, of course, the tunnel." The childhood story was fresh in my memory. "Do you really think it's true?" I extended my dimly lit candle in front of me. I didn't see any tunnel but I hadn't come to the end of the corridor either. If there was in fact a tunnel and if it indeed came out near the church, I would easily be able to navigate towards home.

"It's w-w-worth a try," Thomas said. "My lady, please don't forget about me! You're my only hope. I'm af-f-fraid. I'm af-f-fraid of where they'll send me."

I took a deep breath. "I promise, Thomas. I won't forget. I'll be back and you'll see, everything will be all right."

As I moved further down the corridor, my feet crunched over bits of crushed limestone. Suddenly, along the outer wall, on the left side, a chiseled hole caught my eye. Had I not been looking down to watch my step, I would have missed it! It looked like the opening of a small cave. *Surely this was not the discussed escape route.* I pressed the dimly lit candle into the black hole and found a swirling pit of midnight nothingness. I pulled back and swallowed hard. *Perhaps the getaway Thomas was referring to was further ahead.* I turned and began exploring the corridor in front of me only to discover its abrupt end a short distance away. There was no way out except back from where I came. I returned to the jagged hole in the wall and accepted that it might be the only way to break free. I considered my plan. *If I can't manage, I'll simply crawl back out.* My mind began wildly playing out different scenarios. I sat down, wrapped my skirt between my legs, and wiggled to position myself securely and then I slithered feet first into the mouth of the cave. In the tiny space, I tried to extend my candle but the light wouldn't extend beyond my feet. *What if they were wrong about the tunnel? What if it didn't come out near the church and I ended up lost forever?* As I slowly maneuvered away from the opening, the cave-like tunnel began to feel more like a slide. The downward crest gave my body momentum to keep moving. My chest felt tight with worry, but I kept telling myself that I could return to the top if need be. Although, the more I wriggled and scathed my body against the airless enclosure, the less I trusted in my plan. My legs began to cramp, so I stopped momentarily and turned my head to look up in the direction I'd traveled. I had come a great distance. *How much further?,* I wondered. *Wait. What if I died in here? What have I done?* I didn't know what to do. The air began to swelter making me feel as though my insides might implode from the heat. I didn't know if it was my mind playing tricks on me, but I swore I felt a tapping on my foot. I shook my head. Then, I heard a rustle and something that moved rubbed against the sole of my foot. I jerked my elbow and accidentally extinguished my flame. I blinked hard. Everything was as black as coal. The creature wrestled at my feet and all at once, I felt the skittish thing pounce up my leg and scurry across my arm. Its little claws scraped my neck and, as it swept past my ear, I heard its squeaking cries trail off as it ascended up the tunnel. I could bear it no more. My anguish lurched out as I screamed at the top of my lungs. I couldn't help but thrash about, kicking and screaming, full of panic. Who was this feral creature clawing and scratching at the stone tomb encased around her? *Move,* a hushed voice seemed to whisper over my tangled body. Scooting with slightly bent knees, inch by inch, I progressed deeper into this elusive tunnel. I did not stop, even though I felt throbbing pain shoot through my cramped body. All at once, the ground beneath me gave way. In an instant, I was cascading with intrepid speed through the tunnel. *I am falling.*

Suddenly, I burst out of the cave and into the raven-black night. I tumbled head over heels down a steep ravine, with branches and quagmire whipping my face and body until I finally slid to a halt. *Was I alive?* I wiggled my fingers. I turned my neck from side to side noticing the forest-like trees surrounding me. A barn owl screeched wildly above my head. In response, a cadence of crows cawed in the distance. My body stiffened at the eerie sounds. As I slowly sat up, my head began to pound. I took a deep breath of the cool air; I was alive indeed. I patted my head and then my arms down to my toes, taking inventory of each body part. One of my shoes was missing, but otherwise, I was fairly unscathed. I searched the ground hoping to find my shoe, but was without luck. I heard the sound of trickling water, so I decided to find the source. I hobbled towards the sound and eventually stumbled upon the uneven riverbank, noticing the eclipsed moon cast a purplish reflection over the River Eske as I stood there, thankful to be close to home still. I looked along the water's edge and didn't see the church . . . *perhaps that portion of the story was myth?* Nonetheless, the tunnel had proven to be my escape! I looked up the hill at the dense forest and could barely find the tunnel protruding from the earth.

I kept looking over my shoulder into the dense forest as if someone were watching me. I knew that if I climbed the steep ravine, I could probably find a path through the woods leading me home, but I decided it'd be best if I remained close to the river. I came upon a large tree that had fallen into the river bridging a massive divide and decided to stop and rest.

Suddenly, a brawny voice echoed through the trees, "Who goes there?"

In my haste, I crouched behind the decayed timber. A horse neighed and I wondered who on earth would be riding through the forest at this time of night. The crunching of dried leaves that carpeted the forest floor grew louder. *Oh no, the man was coming to the river! Could he see me?* I squeezed my arms around my legs to form a tighter ball, hoping to remain hidden.

"I said, who goes there?" The strange voice commanded.

I sat motionless with my legs tight against my chest. I could hear the horse splashing water as it clopped along the river's edge. *He was drawing near.* I squeezed my eyes shut because I was too afraid to look. Then I heard the leather saddle creak and the man's feet thud against the earth. His steps grew louder until I felt his toes touching mine. I pried one eye open and saw the gleam from the man's polished boots; they had shiny buckles cinched around his calves. He must be someone important to wear such resplendent boots.

Without warning, his strong hands gripped my shoulders and lifted me up. My feet nearly dangled above the ground as he effortlessly held me up. I'm certain I appeared like a rag doll.

"Honora Katherine Gallagher! Is that you?" His face was flush with mine and I felt his warm breath on the tip of my nose.

"Aye, 'tis I, Honora Gallagher." I thought the bones in my arms might splinter under the pressure of his firm grasp. I let out a small squeak and without warning the man dropped me from his hold.

"Who . . . who are you?" I lifted my chin to question this peculiar man and was struck by his dark stormy eyes. Even under the light of the moon, his handsome complexion appeared swarthy. He possessed a very regal quality—a manner with which I'd never seen anyone carry himself.

The man paused and then let out the most disturbing throated laugh. "I've been searching for you, my dear." The man smirked. "I can't believe I found you."

"What ever do you mean?" I didn't understand his comment.

"I arrive from days on end of exhausting travel and your constable, O'Riley, bombards me with all sorts of precious information, including that you could not be found." The man's chest puffed as he spoke. "Mercy, forgive me. I must extend my condolences for your loss. The favorable news in all of this is that those killers have been apprehended, finally, and now you can move on."

I couldn't even respond to his vulgarity. I just wanted to return home. *Who was this man anyway?*

"Will you *kindly* tell me your name and where you have traveled from?" My teeth grit together as I spoke.

"You do not remember me?" The man flashed a devilish grin. "I am your cousin, Tremore from Waterford."

The man entitled to my inheritance if I failed to comply with the condition to wed. Tremore placed his hands around my arms again, this time as more of an embrace; his touch felt powerful. It was a feeling I've never experienced before.

"Will you allow me to escort you back to the castle?" Tremore took another step towards me, and his finger brushed across my hand as he extended an open hand towards me.

I nodded, feeling speechless.

"Now hurry, we must be getting back. O'Riley is up in arms over your disappearance." Without hesitation, Tremore scooped me up and lifted me onto his horse.

"Rest, my dear. We'll be home soon." Tremore began leading the horse as we made our way through the forest towards the castle. Sheer exhaustion seemed to overcome me, so I bent over the saddle and closed my eyes as the rocking movement lulled my aching body to sleep.

CHAPTER 8

MISS CELIA DUTIFULLY KNOCKED UPON the door of my keep before entering. "'Tis a grand mornin', my lady," she wistfully proclaimed as she placed my breakfast tray upon my desk. I noticed a few more letters tucked beneath the napkin. Miss Celia moved across the room, as though she were floating on clouds, and drew back the mulberry curtains that had puddled on the floor in a velvety swirl. I rubbed my eyes, waking to a soft mercury light that beckoned another day.

I slowly peeled away my coverlet and wiggled towards the edge of my bed. My bum ached and I contemplated the state of my dreadfully sore limbs. The pain reverberated through my body and made me want to howl like a banshee.

Miss Celia's head was stuck in my wardrobe as she thumbed through my clothing selections. *Why was she so giddy?* At least she didn't appear to being coming down with a cold anymore. I wish I shared her enthusiasm for the day; instead I knew that I'd have to plead with O'Riley for Thomas' freedom. Even though the bandits had also been arrested, I needed to understand what proof O'Riley had against Thomas. I grew up with Thomas and I know he loved my father simply by the way he'd followed Pop around like a pup. Perhaps if O'Riley knew the way Thomas took special care to deliver the letter my Pop had written to the Herbert School of Music, he would see that Thomas was good natured.

I also wish I could enlist Leo's help, but after he abandoned me last night in the cellar, I didn't know what to think. It was unlike his character and the thought of this change in behavior made me feel sad.

"What do you think about this one?" Miss Celia said while pulling out the rose-colored dress with the bodice embroidered in a beige lace overlay. Angela had created it for my birthday celebration this year, fashioning it from a design I'd fallen in love with in a Charles Worth advertisement. It seemed especially fancy for a day like today, but I was very fond of wearing it.

"If you think it's best." I pressed my lips together and forced a smile.

"What's the bother?" Miss Celia lowered the dress and took a seat on the bed next to me. "You're slouching. Did you sleep well last night?"

If she only knew. "Nae. It's nothing."

"You can speak plainly to me." Miss Celia's eyes seemed to be searching my face for clues.

"It's O'Riley. I know you've asked me to trust him regarding Thomas and I wish I could. Truthfully though, I'm certain he's making a mistake. Oh, why the bother! He won't listen to me anyways. I suppose he doesn't believe in me because he still sees me as a wee child." My eyes stared at the floor.

"Believe in you?"

"Yeah. Sometimes it feels as though he doesn't believe I'm capable of managing the affairs of the castle. Not that it matters."

"Let me ask you, do you wish to acquire the responsibility of all that Kings Castle has to offer?"

"I didn't think I had much of a choice. I mean, the condition to wed . . ."

"Free will, my lady." Miss Celia rose; carrying the dress in her hand, she moved across the room and delicately laid it on the corner of my bed. "Remember that you will always be given the gift to choose. If you want someone to believe in you, you need to first believe in yourself." As she turned to leave my room, she paused in the doorway and said, "In case you've ever doubted, I believe in you!"

"Well, my dear, aren't you a sight for sore eyes this morning. That dress suits you well," Tremore exclaimed, looking me up and down as I entered the great room. Why was *he* here? I glanced around the room noticing Miss Pavek clearing away some breakfast dishes. O'Riley was positioned next to Tremore whose chest plumped as if he were proud of something.

"Good day, Nora." The tone in O'Riley's greeting felt hard. Distant. There was something different about O'Riley that I couldn't place. Tremore stepped toward me, grabbed my hand and kissed the top of it. "How are you feeling? You took quite the tumble last night." His mischievous grin made me feel uneasy.

"I've had better days." I slid my hand away and felt my face start to flush. "If you don't mind me asking, what are you two doing?" My curiosity spilled over in a high-pitched question.

"Ah, yes, we were simply discussing the transport of our little prisoner." Tremore announced. *Our?* Who did he think he was? I know he was a relative, but it almost seemed as if he were acting as though he lived and reigned here.

I looked at O'Riley and appealed to him, "I . . . I think we've made a mistake. It's Thomas; I believe he's innocent. Will you please wait to transport him until all the evidence—"

"With all due respect, my lady, you do not have all the facts. And without all the facts, your claim of Thomas' innocence has no basis," O'Riley said. "We are certain we have our thief. You should be grateful that justice will be served and we can all move on. Besides, it's too late. Thomas has already been deported."

I felt my breath quicken. *Nae, nae! I promised Thomas I wouldn't leave him. I promised I wouldn't let him down!*

"What? I didn't even get a chance to—"

"I think you had your chance last night," O'Riley said.

"Where is he? I mean, where have you taken him?"

"There, there. Take a deep breath." Tremore placed his clammy hand upon my shoulder and a chill ran through my body. "It's apparent that Thomas meant something awfully special to you and for that I am sorry. If you must know, he has been ushered to the convict depot in Kilmainham. If it's that important to you, I'm sure we could get a message to him from you while he awaits his sentencing . . . isn't that right, O'Riley?" Tremore flashed a determined look in the constable's direction.

O'Riley amused me with an impartial nod.

"Very well. I'll draft a letter for post right away." I turned to Tremore and said, "I'm quite grateful for your sudden interest of the castle affairs, however—"

"Absolutely, my dear," Tremore said. "That is why I have come, to support you and your efforts." He took a step closer, nearly pressing his body into mine and whispered, "Please understand I have vast experience in business and servant affairs. If I were in your position, I would not want to conquer all this alone."

His words were slick: mesmerizing and believable. I heard the sound of footsteps behind me and I turned around to find it was Leo. At first, I felt a rush of anger climb from my spine to the base of my neck. I wanted to beat my chest and demand from him a reason for abandoning me last night. In an instant, that angst hesitated when I caught his expression; his face looked twisted as if he were in pain and his mouth gaped like he'd been insulted. Something was wrong.

"Leo?" I wanted to whisk him into another room and ask what happened.

"My lady." He bowed, keeping his eyes on the floor. "Excuse me, Tremore. Frank's requested that I inform you of your ride into town. He is ready when you are."

"Ah, yes. Thank you, Leo. Please tell him I'll be ready momentarily."

I glanced at O'Riley and Tremore and then back to Leo. He'd already spun around and was nearly about to exit through the front door.

"Wait, Leo, do you mind? I need to ask you—" I looked at Tremore. "Pardon me, I'll be right back." I picked up my skirt and briskly walked into the entrance hall to meet up with Leo where at least we were out of earshot.

"Leo, what happened last night?" I lowered my voice in case anyone tried to eavesdrop. Leo started shaking his head. Still, he wouldn't look me in the eyes.

"I'm terribly sorry."

"You left me! You locked me up in that forbidden . . . "

"It's not what you think. I would never . . . leave you. They startled me and well, I panicked."

"They?"

"Aye. O'Riley and your cousin Tremore." Leo quickly glanced into the other room. "They burst through the kitchen doors and I think they were as shocked as I was to see other people standing there. O'Riley introduced me to Tremore, stating that they wanted to make a late night check on Thomas. I didn't know what to do, so, I slammed the cellar door, bolted it, and made up a story that I'd just come from checking on Thomas, who was fast asleep. As we returned to the gatehouse, O'Riley was out of sorts and began to ask suspicious questions. He wouldn't give up. I broke down and told them it was you, in fact, who was paying a visit to Thomas. Once the truth was out, we came back for you right away. It was too late. You were already gone." Leo lifted his eyes to meet mine and he looked like he was going to cry. "Thomas told us that you'd gone in search of the hidden tunnel. Tremore insisted that he go looking for you. I offered, but O'Riley would not allow it. Apparently, O'Riley knew exactly where the tunnel led and gave Tremore the precise location to find you." Leo's neck hung like a broken branch. "I'm grateful you're all right. I don't know if I'd be able to live with myself . . . "

I put my finger to Leo's lips and a solemn exhale pushed through his teeth; his body seemed to sink.

"I forgive you. It's finished. Now, about Thomas . . . " I leaned back to peer into the great room. O'Riley and Tremore were conversing.

"He's already been sent away, Nora."

"I know. But somehow I need to prove to O'Riley that Thomas is innocent. I think I have an idea," I whispered, thinking that if I could explain how Pop gave Thomas his portfolio after the ambush it might build credibility. "In the meantime, I need you to send a post to Thomas making him aware that I'm at work on his liberation."

A man's cough echoed through the entrance hall. Tremore stood in the entryway and seemed to glare at Leo as he began addressing me. "I'm sorry to disturb your little affair, but I'd best be going. I have some business to conduct from my hotel room." I observed both men and realized that although they possessed very different physical characteristics, each held a very distinguished air about them. Perhaps it was because they appeared to be about the same age. I wasn't sure.

"Before I leave," Tremore affectionately nudged his finger under my chin, "I'm wondering if you would join me this evening for a private dinner? It would suit me fine if you said, yes! After all, it would be good for us to get reacquainted after all these years." Tremore clasped his hands in front of himself and rocked playfully onto his toes.

I quickly examined Leo's face; his jaw was clenched and his eyes were squinted. "Excuse me, my lady," he said, "I'd best be off. I assure you I'll perform your assignment as requested." Then he opened the door and departed the castle before I could respond.

There was so much about Tremore's ambiguous behavior that made me feel conflicted. Perhaps he was right. What harm would come from having dinner together? Maybe if I spent a little time getting to know him, I would discover what was hidden behind his dramatic expressions and eager motivation toward Kings Castle.

"I suppose I owe you a proper meal for all you've done." My stomach felt like it was doing somersaults.

"Grand, perhaps you shall accompany me this evening? Let's say seven o'clock at the Abbey Hotel." He leaned in and kissed my cheek before leaving. As the door closed behind him, I felt a rush of cold air sweep through the room.

The Abbey Hotel was popular among business travelers. Its delightful owners, David and Shannon Ellison, had earned themselves a favorable reputation for good hospitality. It was too bad their daughter, Violet, didn't share those same attributes.

I tied Snow to the hitching post outside the hotel. The two-story stone building was all aglow. *They must be fully occupied this evening.* I took a deep breath, hoping Violet wasn't around to help her parents this evening. I pushed open the front door and triggered the bell that hung around the knob. In the sitting room to the left of the entrance, there were a handful of unfamiliar men conversing. My arrival issued a brief silence and I could feel their stares, which made me feel like my clothes were suddenly on fire. I was certain that word of my inheritance had carried throughout the countryside on the wings of the westerly wind, making Kings Castle—and myself in particular—the talk of the county. I kept my focus straight ahead. Shannon Ellison rounded the corner, her apron tied around her waist.

"Why Honora, what a pleasure to see you! We were told to expect you this evening."

"Aye. 'Tis a grand night when one gets to enjoy a lovely meal prepared by the one and only, Shannon Ellison. I believe my cousin, Tremore Gallagher, is staying with you while he is in town?"

"Indeed. An impressionable man, he is," Shannon spoke fondly. There was definitely something of intrigue about Tremore Gallagher, and it struck me that I wasn't the only one to take notice. Shannon escorted me to the library, a quaint room down the short hall. As I entered, Tremore was sitting with two other men whose backs were to me. In unison, the three men stood to greet me when I walked in. *Oh.* Those other men were Lawrence and Steven Aiken. I'd forgotten that they too were staying at the Abbey Hotel. I wondered how they knew each other since the Aikens were from Lifford and Tremore was from Waterford—opposite ends of the country.

"You look absolutely stunning, my dear." Tremore had a rogue look in his eyes. "I believe you've already met the Aiken brothers." He placed his hand upon the small of my back to escort me into their circle.

"What a lovely surprise gentlemen. I hadn't expected to see you here since, well, I thought after the announcement that your work here was complete." I pressed my fingers over my lips attempting to mask the bitter taste in my mouth. "I can see you know one another." I regarded each man with a glance.

"Indeed," Steven replied. "Our law firm has had a long standing relationship with the Gallagher clan over the years. We know Tremore quite well. I'm sure you can understand how important it is that we follow the proper procedure when it comes to informing a person who's been named in a Trust of their potential rights and inheritance."

"That is in part the reason we invited Tremore to Donegal Town," Lawrence said. "You have nothing to worry about, Honora. We've taken the liberty to explain to Tremore what's at stake in regards to your father's estate."

Ach! How I ached for the innocence of the way life used to be. But here I was faced with trying to understand the tangled web of legal matters and discerning the motives of others. I felt stuck in a moment that I desperately wanted to escape. Realizing that there was no way out made me feel like I had the other night, trapped. I shook my head.

"Very well." I wasn't well. In fact, I felt my insides twist and knot as if I'd swallowed a ball of twine. "Shall you be joining us for dinner?"

"Thank you for the offer, my lady," Steven said, "We already have plans this evening."

"Aye, a fundraising event to support George Sigerson's new relief committee," Lawrence chimed in.

George Sigerson? Where had I heard this name before? Oh, yes! He was part of the group trying to help the poor Irish tenants who'd been suffering through this year's famine. I suppose it was a good thing these men were supporting an honorable cause, at least I'm sure Pop would agree since he found favor with the work of this organization.

Just as Shannon Ellison returned to invite Tremore and me to our table, the Aiken brothers bid us farewell, encouraging me to send a post if I needed anything. Tremore and I turned to follow Shannon toward the back of the hotel and into a small parlor room. A lit candle adorned the center of a linen covered table nestled against a large window. We walked to the table and Tremore pulled out the chair so that I could sit with my back against the window. Mrs. Ellison filled our crystal glasses with water and left the room.

Once we were alone, I began to feel squeamish. Perhaps this is what the Princess from the fable *The Princess and the Pea* felt like: uncomfortable from the wrongful placement of something hidden. It sure felt like I was being tested too. Who was this man, after all?

"You'll have to forgive me, Tremore. I don't remember much about you at all."

"'Tis a shame it's taken a tragedy to bring us together. I believe the last time we were together was when our Grandmam passed. You were a wee child then, which would explain your poor memory." Tremore winked. "Now look at you—all grown up and ravishingly beautiful."

A sudden itch on my leg caused me to squirm. "Perhaps you could start by telling me about your work?" I desperately wanted to shift the conversation away from Tremore's thoughts about my appearance.

He nodded enthusiastically. "I operate a music academy. It was the family business and I took over after my father's passing. For the past several years, I have been traveling around the world, contracting with musicians who wish to perform on stage or in great halls. I've been quite busy, which I hope excuses my absence of visiting you, my dear." Tremore's voice rang with impressive confidence.

I couldn't believe it. A music academy? My dream! How could this be? This man, next in line should I fail to uphold the condition . . . could this be fate? Who was I kidding? My life was dull in comparison to my cousin, Tremore. To this point, I had no good work to boast of. Clearly, it seemed he was the more qualified person to inherit the property. *How could Pop have declared that I gain first rights to Kings Castle?*

"Since the Aikens have disclosed all the details surrounding my, um, inheritance, I'm curious, how do you feel about the possibility of being named as the benefactor should I fail."

Tremore reached across the table and grasped my hand, which sent a shiver down my spine. "Listen, my dear. You deserve the right to remain in your home. It seems rather simple to me."

"Oh? Because I feel very confused. Very . . . um, uncertain. The tasks, demands, and decisions that would be required of me. To be perfectly honest, I think you would be more suitable to handle the affairs."

"'Tis impossible to fail so long as you adhere to the stipulation that you wed within the year." Tremore casually took a sip from his glass.

Shannon appeared from around the corner pushing a cart that carried tonight's meal. She placed a loaf of soda bread in front of us.

"Your dress is beautiful," Shannon complimented me as she set a plate of her renowned cabbage rolls in front of me. "It reminds me of something Queen Victoria would wear."

"Thank you, Mrs. Ellison. That is a very gracious thing for you to say."

I glanced across the table and caught Tremore rolling his eyes.

"Now, where were we?" Tremore interrupted.

"My apologies." I saw Shannon's neck turn florid. "Enjoy your meal!" she mumbled as she scooted out of the room.

I fumbled with my fork and took a few bites.

"I've been thinking," Tremore pushed his plate of food away and leaned back in his chair. "We should get married."

CHAPTER 9

"HONORA GALLAGHER, WILL YOU MARRY me?" Tremore repeated.

The notion was inconceivable. I didn't want to get married to Tremore—or anyone for that matter. Not yet, anyway. Until the condition had been made known, I'd believed my future was all about attending the Herbert School of Music. Since Pop died, everything in my life was changing so quickly and the future felt uncertain. It was as though everything that was once familiar to me was becoming a distant memory. I'd wanted to return to playing Lover with joyful adoration, but as of late, all I could muster was staring at her with a fond remembrance, as if she were a stranger. Every ambition seemed stripped away.

Tremore leaned back in his chair with a confident grin streaking his face.

"I . . . um, I'm not sure what to say." I moved the silverware around on the table. "I have a lot of things on my mind these days. I might need some time to—"

"Say yes!" Tremore slid his hand over mine. "It's quite simple. Let me help ease your mind."

Somehow I wasn't convinced. I needed to sort through the muddled thoughts. I needed time. Ah, yes. *Time.* A tickle in my throat caused me to cough. "I need a wee bit of time. 'Tis a big decision and, well, I'm sure you understand."

Tremore's lower lip curled. "My dear, you realize that this 'time' you speak of is your enemy. The clock is ticking." He released a slight groan. "Nevertheless, my affection for you remains, and when you come to the proper realization that my offer is true, I will be waiting."

To my relief, Shannon appeared again in the doorway. "Excuse me, my lady, but you've some visitors who've requested to see you."

"Oh?" Leo was the only one who'd overheard of my dinner plans this evening. "Who is it, if may I ask?"

"John and Angela O'Doolan. I've invited them to wait in the sitting room."

"Very well, thank you, Mrs. Ellison."

Tremore accompanied me into the sitting room.

"Angela?" I surveyed the emptied room, feeling relieved that the other guests from earlier in the evening had dispersed. "What are you doing—wait, how did you know I was here?"

"Sorry to trouble you. We didn't know you . . ." Angela peered at Tremore who was standing behind me. "John and I were passing through town when we noticed Snow hitched outside." Angela gestured towards the front window.

"Nae, nae bother at all. Your timing is . . . great." I coughed as that tickle returned. "John and Angela, I'd like to introduce you to my cousin, Tremore." I waved my hand in an overly dramatic fashion.

"Angela is our housemaid and castle seamstress. 'Tis her lovely hands to thank for making this dress you seem to like so well." I placed my hands upon my hips and smiled, but Tremore didn't smile back. His sudden displeasure hung like a cockeyed picture on the wall.

"And . . . em, this is her husband John who handles all the trades for the castle. Their families have worked for us for many years," I explained.

Tremore turned his nose up. "Greetings. It's a pleasure to meet a few more of the servants for Kings Castle. To what do we owe your unexpected drop in?"

"Our apologies, my lord," John said quickly, "We were passing through town on our way to"—his eyes darted to Angela—"a social gathering." It wasn't difficult to decipher Angela's mood; clenched fists, puckered cheeks, and glaring eyes spoke of her irritation.

"The crossroads," Angela exclaimed. "There's a dance tonight at the crossroads and we thought we'd see if you cared to join us." John began rubbing the back of his neck as if he were plagued with bed bugs. I'm sure Angela's forthright announcement made him feel uncomfortable, especially since no one really seemed to know anything about Tremore. What was his position on these sorts of things?

The crossroads—the intersection of two country roads—were only a short distance from town. One dusty road led east toward the O'Riley farm and the other was a narrow road that spiraled north toward more rugged terrain. It'd been a longtime meeting place for dances under the canopy of the moon and the stars. The crossroads location was secluded enough so that we'd be less likely to disturb the opinions of folks who forbid activities such as dancing and music. I'd been going to the crossroads for years, in secret, of course. It was fun; it didn't bother me at all that I was linking arms with someone who might be viewed by the gentry as a different social class than me. However, clearly, someone like Tremore might find offense in my participation.

"Oh. I think that sounds—"

Tremore pulled me aside. "Are you thinking of leaving with the likes of these people?" he whispered. "You realize their type is not like ours. It'd be wise if you were a bit more mindful of your responsibility to the castle. 'Tis never a good thing to mix your affairs with that of the common tenant."

There it was; his position would not favor mine, as I'd suspected. "I understand what you're saying but these people are more than common tenants to me. They're friends too." I paused, taking a moment to relax my shoulders. "I don't see anything wrong with enjoying a little entertainment." Affirming those thoughts gave me a sense of freedom. "Thank you for your concern, Tremore. I'm awfully sorry if you disapprove, but . . . I think I could withstand a wee bit of enjoyment tonight." It felt good to speak my mind. "You're welcome to join me, if you wish."

I stepped away from his hold on my arm.

Turning toward Angela I said, "I'd be delighted to join you."

Tremore deliberated, his eyes stared at the corner of the room as if he were calculating his thoughts. "There, there, don't be leavin' in such a flurry," he said. "I've pledged to spend the evening with you and I'd be obliged to go along with you."

I wondered why Tremore would choose to come despite his feelings. Did he really care about what I thought? Angela threw her shoulders back as she marched out the door.

"All right then, if you wish," I said.

Once outside, John hitched Snow to the team pulling the wagon. The brilliant moon illuminated the countryside as we traveled. Whenever the night was bright, it made the prospect of a crossroads dance even more exciting. There was always more to see and feel on a night such as tonight. A short distance out of town I could see a small flicker of light nestled into the hillside. It was coming from the O'Donnell farmhouse, another plot of land owned by Kings Castle. Leo grew up on this farm. His da and ma had been tenants for as long as I was alive. I'm not sure what happened, but something caused Leo to decide at a young age that he wanted to leave farming behind to pursue a more distinguished life. Red O'Riley helped him earn the gatekeeper position as a new start.

As the wagon lurched further down the road, we began to hear the sounds of laughter and the subtle twang of a banjo. We were getting close. I jerked when Tremore abruptly put his arm around me. Was this his way of lightening the mood? I wondered why Tremore was so intense all the time. Perhaps the crossroads would help him to unwind. Maybe then, we could begin the start of a decent relationship.

As we neared the intersection, John pulled the reigns to stop the team a short distance from the gathering.

"There are a lot of folks out tonight and I'd prefer to keep the team at a distance. Do you mind walking a wee bit?" John inquired. I caught the faint sound of someone's banjo being played in a high-pitched warble. Loud stomping and clapping wafted in the dewy air.

"That's grand, John. Nae bother here. We've all got healthy legs, right, Tremore?" I nudged his side playfully.

John helped Angela down from the wagon and together they walked toward the festivities. I couldn't move because Tremore's arm was still clasped around me.

"Are ya comin'?" Angela turned and called out to me.

"Aye, you go on ahead." I glanced at Tremore suspiciously. "We'll be following right behind you."

As they disappeared down the gravel road, I turned my attention toward Tremore. His expression had slightly changed and I couldn't help but notice the way his lip snarled, as if he were a dog preparing to fight.

"Is something wrong?" I questioned, wondering if I'd made a mistake in inviting him.

He shook his head and that look of entanglement slowly erased from his face. "Shall we?" Tremore hopped down from the wagon, turning to offer his hand.

Tonight the crossroads were full of townsfolk. Most were considerably close to my age and, well, most were unmarried. The music being played by the three-piece band caused nearly everyone to dance and sing along to the reel, kicking up a cloud of dust. A few lanterns hung from stakes that'd been pounded into the ground. Their glow seemed to kindle the low-lying haze.

Tremore took a handkerchief from his pocket and covered his nose and mouth. That prideful demeanor I was growing accustomed to was written all over his face.

"Is this the entertainment you hoped for, my dear?" Tremore asked condescendingly.

Ugh. He frustrated me at the moment. I'd been trying everything to make him feel at ease and he responded this way? "It was your notion to come along, so please stop troubling me with your sighs and frowns." I shrugged off his hold and I turned to walk into the sea of people. As I moved deeper into the crowd it seemed that a pathway began to part before me. Did the conversations seem to lull or was it my imagination? I did my best to act nonchalant, like I belonged, but doubt crept into my mind with each passing step. Who was I kidding? I'd never fit in, no matter how hard I tried. I'd always be considered different. I could hear the whispers in my head. *Too good,* some would say. Others, *'tis a shame.* I felt a slight tap on my shoulder and I turned to see Leo hovering over me. His dimpled grin, brimming from ear to ear, instantly seemed to settle my anxiousness. It was good to see him smile.

"Hey." Leo's soft green eyes landed on mine. "I'm surprised to see you here. I thought you were going out with that Tree Man tonight."

"Huh?" *Who was he talking about?* "Ach! You mean, Tremore?" I chuckled. It felt good to laugh. "Yeah, we did. I mean—" I stood on my tiptoes to look through the crowd in the direction I'd just come, but I couldn't see Tremore anywhere.

"Who are you—?" Leo dodged a look in the same direction. "Ah. Tree Man is here, isn't he?"

I nodded, and I felt my face crinkle as if I'd sucked on a lemon. It was hard to mask my disapproval.

He continued, "Well, I've had a productive night, kid." I tried to keep focused on what Leo was saying, but something seemed different about him. "I met with O'Riley this evening and have been able to uncover a great deal tonight regarding the stolen money." Leo shoved his hands into the pockets of his suit coat. *That was it!* Leo was wearing a suit coat. I'd grown so accustomed to his uniform.

"You're fooling me! How were you able to discover this information so quickly?" I looked over my shoulder—I was worried that Tremore would encroach upon the conversation at any moment. "Tell me. Tell me everything you know!"

Leo bit his lip. “It’s not good. O’Riley and the garda were able to recover most of the missing money from the home of one of those attackers.”

“Oh, really? But that’s good news!”

“Except, they also discovered correspondence between Thomas and the bandits. He was behind the plot after all.”

I shook my head. “But why?”

“It’s hard to know. Money troubles, perhaps. Money makes people do strange things. Like I said, we’re living in desperate times in this land of ours.”

“I believed him, I really did.”

“You said you needed the proof. This is it, kid. I know this is hard to comprehend right now.” Leo combed his fingers through his ruddy-blond hair. “I guess O’Riley was onto something with Thomas—something you and I couldn’t see. But like my ma always said, 'Darkness will always have its day.' Leo looked off toward the farmhouse silhouette carved into the moonlit hillside. “I think she meant that God is always working to expose the hidden things of night with the light of day. Let me ask you, has O’Riley ever proven that he cannot be trusted?”

I contemplated Leo’s question. As far as I could remember, he’d always been steadfast to the castle. Pop trusted him, so I should too. And, he’d never shown himself to be dishonest. “Nae.”

“Then I believe we ought to trust him, okay?” Leo reached for my hand and without hesitation pressed his lips onto the top of my hand.

I nodded, choosing to accept what I didn’t completely understand. Leo’s kindness warmed my heart.

I surveyed the folks carrying on around us. Angela was clinging to John as they danced a set.

"Leo, this song is *When the Sun Sinks to Rest* by Samuel Lover!"

"Well then, may I have this dance?" Leo lifted the palm of his hand in the air as a free offering to take if I pleased.

"You may." I wrapped my fingers around his and I felt Leo's hand rest on my hip. As we danced, we sang along to the melody:

When the sun sinks to rest,
And the star of the west
Sheds its soft silver light o'er the sea;
What sweet thoughts arise,
As the dim twilight dies—
For then I am thinking of thee!

When we finished, my heart felt full. I couldn't remember the last time I'd laughed and enjoyed the company of another as much as tonight. However, slowly, the sinking realization that I'd abandoned Tremore caused my insides to flutter with slight anticipation.

"I'd best be going, Leo. Thank you for all the kindness you've shown me tonight. I didn't realize how desperate I was for some jolly good fun. Even though I'm disappointed with the turn of events regarding Thomas, this evening surely has helped to take my mind off of my grief . . . for the time being anyway."

I left Leo and began heading toward the outer circle. I had barely put one foot in front of the other when I noticed him off in the distance piercing me with his dark eyes. I squinted through the haze. Tremore's glaring eyes were glued to me. I sighed. *Why did he exhaust me?* Part of me wished he'd leave. Perhaps, in a few days, he would return to his own home. Then I remembered his proposal. *Ugh.* I wondered if anything good would come of this.

"Whatever seems to be the problem, my lord?" I asked.

"Ha! It seems that I am not the one with the problem." Tremore turned his back to me and began walking down the road in the direction of the wagon. As I began to follow him, Angela shouted to me from the crowd, "Honora! Are you ready to depart?"

I waved her off. "Nae, 'tis a great night for a walk!" I hurried to catch up to Tremore's side.

"Do you have any idea what a pity it is to see the castle put to such shame?" His words were muted by the wind. "You have been given the opportunity to rule and reign; instead, you shrink back from your duty and befriend the likes of *these* . . . people!"

"Excuse me?"

He stopped abruptly, twisting himself to face me. Poking his finger towards my face he said, "You allowed that—that servant boy over there to touch and kiss you! It's quite fair to say that you have forgotten who you are. If only your father could see what you've become. 'Tis a disgrace!"

Tears began to well up within me, and I had an urge to run and hide. I clenched my fists and choked on the lump that'd risen in my throat. The weight of worthlessness crushed my chest. I put my head down. *Don't cry . . . don't cry . . . don't cry.*

I picked up my skirt and began to stomp away from Tremore. I needed to escape. Picking up pace, I decided I would head straight to the castle on my own, even if it took me all night—so long as Tremore Gallagher would leave me be. As I reached the wagon I doubled over, heaving for air. I looked over my shoulder and could see Tremore's shadow remained still. I turned to keep going and collided with Leo. I screamed, startled with shock.

"What's the trouble?" Leo said.

"Leo, how did you . . .?" I gasped for breath. "He . . . won't leave." I clasped my hands to my face but they couldn't stop the flood of tears.

"Honora Gallagher!" Tremore's voice called out.

My whole being tensed when I heard Tremore's voice, causing me to bury my face deeper into the lapel of Leo's suit coat and he held me up. From behind I could hear the crunching sound of gravel scuff against boots. A silence covered my ears as though I were wearing muffs on a cold winter's day. Had the music stopped playing?

I became utterly still, my tears halted. When I lifted my face from my hands I witnessed the oddest thing. Leo had extended one hand, his palm facing Tremore, who was standing a short distance away. It appeared as though Tremore's lip was curled, the same defiant look as when we first arrived.

Tremore insisted, "Let me take you home, Honora. We can sort through all this misunderstanding another time."

"You shouldn't go with him," Leo whispered, tugging me closer to his side. "I'll help you with Snow, and I can escort you to the castle. You can tell him to leave!"

I felt so weak. All my inadequacies were piling up like a graveyard of bones. There was no hiding the truth of Tremore's words. He was right—surely, I was a disgrace to the castle, and my ignorance proved it.

"I don't think I can."

"Listen to me," Leo said, lifting my chin to look at him. "You can! You have the authority to command a great deal of things. All you need to do is speak it out loud so he can hear you clearly."

"But he won't listen to me."

"I assure you, he will listen!"

I contemplated my options. Leave with Tremore or allow Leo to help me? After such a hurtful exchange, I wondered how there could ever be any reconciliation between Tremore and myself. The thought of staying with Leo made me feel comforted, like he was taking care of me as my father once did, and I felt an unusual confidence gird itself from somewhere within. "Tremore, you need to go!" I demanded, bracing my spirit for a backlash.

I was shocked when Tremore, without a word, turned and disappeared into the black of night.

I couldn't shake his words: *it's quite fair to say that you have forgotten who you are. If only your father could see what you've become.* I began to tear up again at the notion. Was I a disappointment to my father? Of course, I wanted to make him proud of me. Who was I becoming?

CHAPTER 10

I AWOKE FROM A DEEP sleep to the sound of feet padding across my bedchamber floor. I watched as Miss Celia quietly hoisted the wooden letterbox onto my writing desk. I promptly sat up to gain a better view.

"I'm terribly sorry to wake you, my lady. I hoped to slip in and out without disturbing yer rest."

"What's in the box?" I rubbed my eyes.

Miss Celia paused. She picked up a handful of letters and fanned them in the air.

"Oh." I rolled my eyes.

"It appears every viable man in the county, or maybe even the country, would like a fair hand in yer selection process."

"Unfortunately."

"This arrived for you too." She plucked a smaller envelope from the stack.

I leaned forward, straining to read the words scrawled across the paper, then lifted the palm of my hand. "May I?"

Miss Celia handed me the note, then turned her attention to my wardrobe. I quickly opened the envelope. The signature seemed to leap off the page. *Tremore.*

Dearest Honora,

My apologies regarding our recent misunderstanding. I do hope you can forgive my rather brash behavior. I regret to inform you that I've received word that my business is in need of my prompt return due to an unforeseen circumstance. I hope you understand that I'm unable to be with you at this time. In the meantime, I hope you'll seriously consider my proposal for marriage.

Until we meet again,

Tremore

I whipped the note onto my bed and fell back into my pillow. I didn't want to look at his name, much less think about having to choose a suitor. It didn't seem fair. This wasn't the way things were supposed to turn out, and yet Tremore was causing me to face the harsh reality: sooner or later, I would need to tell these beloved people that I was not going to marry. *It's been my life's ambition to play music and that's what I ought to do.* Surely, when I explained the letter my Pop had written on my behalf in his final days, everyone would understand. Ach! Why did this need to be so challenging? At least Tremore was gone, for now. I took a deep breath feeling a sense of relief that I wouldn't have to face his headlong inquisitions while I sorted through my thoughts.

"Can I talk to you about something weighing on my heart?" I swung my legs out from under the covers and let my feet dangle off the side of the bed.

"Of course." Miss Celia laid out my day dress before taking a seat in the chair. She folded her hands into her lap giving me her full attention. Her face appeared soft and peaceful.

"Let's say, perhaps, I were to go away for a little while . . . " Miss Celia's eyes slowly opened, growing wide like the courtyard's yawning tulips. "How shall I say this?" I chewed on my lip. "I've decided that I'm going to the Herbert School of Music. It's the right choice, for me."

Miss Celia gave me a hungry stare as if she were waiting for the next course to be served.

"Wouldn't you agree?" I prodded.

Miss Celia grew taller in her seat. "I suppose that's what you'd call free will, Honora."

"Free will?

"These conditions you've been placed under have demanded a great deal from you in the way of making decisions for yer future. You can no longer abide in that childlike state. You're coming into yer own, which I believe has been masterfully orchestrated, as it should. I also understand that making the right decisions in life can be awfully hard. But that's the beauty in free will. 'Tis one of God's greatest gifts to humanity. It demonstrates His deep love for His people to show us the very nature of His character, that He is not forceful. Rather He delights in giving us the freedom to choose."

"So you're saying that it doesn't matter what I choose?"

"Surely, it matters. Life is all about choices—both good and bad. 'Tis more about knowing that if you trust God to be faithful and you look to Him in all yer ways, He will guide yer path."

There it was again, the notion of God's faithfulness. Sure, I believed in God. I mean, that's what I was taught. But the idea of trusting Him was hard because of all He'd taken away from me.

"What I'm trying to explain, Honora, is that you can choose to wed or you can choose to leave the castle for music school. Wherever you go, God will go with you. It took me a while to acknowledge Him in all things and I wish I'd learned that lesson much earlier in my life, but, if you truly seek God in yer decisions, He will make straight yer path."

Miss Celia walked over to my desk and began to dig through the letterbox, lifting a book from beneath its contents.

"What is that?"

Miss Celia carried it across the room and handed it to me. "It's a gift, for you."

I held the thick, black, leather-bound book and ran my fingers over the gold embossed letters on the cover. It was a Bible.

"'Twas your mother's."

My Mam's Bible? I couldn't believe it. I'd never been given anything that belonged to my Mam. I opened the cover and inscribed on the first page was a name and date that read:

With love: Asenath Nicholson, 1848

"Who is Asenath Nicholson?"

"She was before yer time. Asenath was a pioneer, of sorts, who devoted her love and attention to Ireland's poor. She was an American, actually. But when she became widowed at a young age, she said God put a burden on her heart to distribute Bibles in Ireland. She was a one-woman relief operation. When she first arrived, she started a soup kitchen in Dublin. Then, shortly after she began walking through the countryside reading Scripture and giving Bibles as gifts in the different towns she came to. That's how yer Mam met her. When yer Mam was but a wee child, Asenath's travels brought her through yer Mam's village. Yer Mam listened to Asenath's stories and Scripture reading and was then given this Bible before Asenath left town." Miss Celia took a seat next to me on the bed. "I was sorting through some of yer father's belongings and came across it. I guess he kept it, knowing how much yer mother treasured it."

"She did?"

"Aye. Yer Mam loved God's Word. She never said, but I think the encounter with Asenath Nicholson really impacted her life for good." Miss Celia patted my back, "I know yer mother would want this passed onto you. 'Twas part of her legacy . . . and now, it can be part of yours too."

I sat still for a moment, feeling the weight of this precious gift upon my lap. It certainly was a treasure, indeed. I thumbed the pages and opened it at random, landing in the book of Isaiah. A verse underlined in pencil caught my eye:

"Though the mountains be shaken and the hills be removed,
yet my unfailing love for you will not be shaken
nor my covenant of peace be removed,"
says the Lord, who has compassion on you.

I wondered why my Mam underlined these words.

Miss Celia closed her eyes. I watched her chest deflate as she slowly exhaled, and she held a fist to her mouth and cleared her throat. Then Miss Celia lifted her head and said, "I understand you want to spread yer wings. You're at the age . . . " A knock at the door interrupted her statement. She stepped to open the door and Angela peeked her head in the room. "I'm sorry to disturb you, Honora, but there's someone here to see you. He says he's an acquaintance, goes by the name Albert Edward Cooper."

As I entered the great room, Albert Edward was standing with his back to me, looking out the window at the courtyard below.

"Good day, Mr. Cooper," I said.

Albert Edward turned toward me. He was dressed in a brightly colored uniform and his red pants were tucked into tall, shiny black boots. Over his shoulder, through the window, I noticed a tall black horse stationed outside the gatehouse. At a distance, Leo and Frank were engaged in conversation.

He stepped toward me. "Lady Nora." He pressed his lips to my extended hand. "It's a pleasure to see you again." Albert Edward's hand was slightly trembling. Was he nervous? "I apologize if I've disrupted any of your plans for the day by calling unannounced."

"Nae bother." I waved my hands in the air attempting to mask my arousing suspicion regarding his abrupt arrival. "Tell me, what brings you to Kings Castle?" I felt a surge of panic rush through my body, hoping he didn't inquire about his most recent letter since I hadn't read it.

"Ah, yes. I'm on a venture, of sorts, for my father's charity organization, The Mansion House Relief. I've been charged to investigate the deplorable conditions of a nearby island that the committee hopes to deliver aid to. But before I continue my travels westward, I've arranged to rest for a wee couple days at our country home. I've thought about you a considerable bit since we first met, to which, I hope you don't mind me taking the liberty of requesting your company this afternoon. I wondered if you might consider joining me on a ride."

I took another peek out the window before responding. "Ach! I don't know if I—"

"She's an ol' mare," his voice quivered.

"Huh?"

"Margy." He thumbed towards his horse in the courtyard. "About as unstable as the political climate. It's her age. In fact, if it wasn't for her, I might have arrived a whole day earlier." Albert Edward let out a throated laugh that made me jump.

"Oh. I see." Perhaps this was Albert Edward's strange way of carrying on a conversation.

"But she's been a part of my life since I was a wee one. I'm sure it sounds like nonsense, keepin' her around, but the ol' mare is like kin to me. It's funny the ways in which we grow a bond with these animals of ours. Oh bother, there I go again, speakin' for myself." Albert Edward slapped his leg, sending a shrill of nervous laughter through the room.

I understood the affection towards a person's animal. "Oh, it makes perfect sense to me. I have a connection with my first mare too. Snow is her name. I couldn't imagine a ride without her."

"Ah, yes." Albert Edward delivered a warbled laugh. "It sounds as if we'd make a good pair. So, you'll join me?"

I felt my face burn up like a fever. He seemed to be a very kind man, odd for sure, but gracious. What harm could come from a leisurely ride?

"I suppose some fresh air and an afternoon jaunt would fair well for me."

"That's grand. Certainly having the pleasantry of your company will fair me well too."

While Frank prepared Snow for riding, I quickly changed into a more suitable habit. Upon my return, as I entered the courtyard, both Margy and Snow were positioned near the gatehouse. Albert Edward walked across the grounds, extending his hand to escort me. In a bizarre sort of way, I rather enjoyed his attention. Albert Edward wasn't pushy or rude. He was different, but kind. As we approached the horses, Leo, who'd been guarding the gate nearby, marched up to us.

"I understand you'll be venturing off this afternoon with Mr. Cooper." Leo tipped his hat at Albert Edward. A peculiar spark streaked across his eyes as if a star had fallen from the sky. No sooner had I seen it, the expression was gone. "Is there anything you'll be needing from me?"

"Thank you, Leo. We'll be gone only for a brief excursion. Would you kindly tell Miss Pavek I'll be home in time for dinner?"

"Very well." Leo hesitated as if he wanted to say more.

"May I?" Albert Edward stepped in, offering his hand to help me mount Snow. Leo's mouth fell. I suppose he was accustomed to offering his assistance. I took the reigns as Albert Edward got situated on Margy. I regarded Leo as he ambled to his post and began maneuvering the gate open for our departure.

Albert Edward led us away from town, along a worn trail cut through the hillside. The tall grass on either side of us hid the various rocks and piles of stones scattered intermittently. The sky looked like a thick portrait of gray pointillism. At any moment, I imagined that the tiny speckles blanketing the sky would begin misting the earth.

Feeling the need to say something, I said, "Tell me about yourself. I mean, I know your father is the Lord Lieutenant of Ireland and he is a huge proponent of serving the poor, particularly through the Mansion House Relief."

"Ah, yes! My father." Albert Edward's lips pressed together. "My identity." He released a piercing laugh.

I leaned toward Albert Edward. "Is this a sore subject for you?"

"You know, his responsibilities are grand. A duty he reminds me of every day," Albert Edward said. "I hate to admit it, but I leap at the chance to travel without him. Anything to escape the tyranny of his blasted regime for performance and perfection." He stole a quick glance in my direction and I offered a sad smile.

"I understand how you feel." Although my circumstance was different, I assuredly empathized with his frustration.

"I'm sorry, it's awfully rude of me to be speaking in such tones before the lovely Nora Gallagher. I promise I won't mention my grievances again."

For a considerable distance we moseyed along, side by side, without saying a word. Finally I said, "So, when do you depart for your business assignment?"

"Tomorrow," Albert Edward replied. "You're familiar with the work of the Mansion House Relief Committee? To help alleviate the desolate conditions among the poor in Ireland?"

"My father was involved, I believe. I know he was actively trying to raise money for their efforts, but I don't know exactly what they do to help the poor."

"They take reported cases of destitution in villages, solicit for benevolence, and supply food or other care items to aid the village inhabitants' health. You ought to join me."

"Huh?"

"I'll be traveling on behalf of the Committee to Moore Island. I'm to report the islanders' living conditions to determine if support should be ordered. Perhaps you'd like to experience firsthand the work your father invested in?"

Was Albert Edward inviting me to travel with him on his business assignment? How could it be? Surely, this was not the time to leave the castle for an extended period.

"It sure seems like quite the grand idea, but I don't know if . . . "

"We'd be away only for a couple weeks—a rather quick trip. But I do have one little problem."

"Oh?"

"It's my footman. He's come down with that terrible sickness that's been spreading in these parts. I was relying on his assistance, but now, it appears I need to find myself another hired hand. The problem is that I'm not from these parts. Do you have a recommendation for me?"

"A hired hand?" I bit my cheek. "Oh, yes. I know someone who could help you. His name is Jack Griffith, a Traveling fellow."

"A Traveler?" Albert Edward began to wheeze. He nearly fell off Margy in unruly laughter. If I hadn't noticed his wide grin, I might not have been able to remain so calm. Albert Edward's queer behaviors were becoming more normal to me. "That's grand! My father would absolutely disapprove of hiring someone of that untrustworthy nature."

Was he joking? My words pushed through my clenched jaw, "Well, Mr. Cooper, I've known Jack Griffith my whole life. Pop hired him for odd jobs all the time and he is not the sort of man that you are making him out to be. In fact, I'm deeply offended that you would suggest—"

"My lady, I said my father would disapprove." Albert Edward sucked another breath. "*I* am not my father. If Mr. Griffith is an honest, hard-working fellow, then I gleefully accept your recommendation." Albert Edward beamed. "So what do you say? Will you accept my invitation?"

I couldn't sleep. I'd said yes to Albert Edward's request and spent the previous two days making arrangements for travel. I still couldn't believe Miss Celia complied with me going on this adventure. Surely, I'd believed she was going to resist the notion, but to my surprise she went along with it, so long as the measures for proper etiquette were in place. She was transforming before my very eyes. In preparation, Miss Celia had arranged for Angela to accompany me as my lady maid, and she even went so far as to line up the working agreement with Jack Griffith.

I tossed and turned in bed a while longer before deciding to get up for the day. Perhaps I would make myself a light snack while I waited, as there were a still a few hours of night before dawn, our appointed meeting time to leave.

As I approached the kitchen, I noticed a soft glow protruding through the crack of the door. *That was odd.* I pushed open the door and saw Leo sitting at the table. He jumped slightly, standing instinctively at my entrance.

"Leo, what in the world are you doing up at this hour?" I asked.

"'Tis as good a question for you, kid."

"It looks like we have the same idea." I nodded, poking my nose at his plate with a slice of cheese and broken bread.

"Would you like me to get you a plate?" he asked.

"Nae, you go on and finish eating."

Leo returned to his seat as I slid my Gladstone bag and Lover under the table. Leo squinted his eyes, giving me a look of curiosity. I sat down in the chair opposite him. Tearing a small piece of bread from the loaf on the table I began to chew slowly.

Leo pulled out his pocket watch. "Mind telling me what you've got cookin' at this hour?"

As I started to answer, bread lodged itself in my throat, and in a moment I was choking. I held my hands to my neck. Every time I sucked for breath, sand-like particles of breadcrumbs filtered down my airway. I spun around, looking for some water. I was beginning to feel desperate. As my arms began flapping, Leo mimicked the gesture and shouted, "What! Water? You need water?"

I nodded my head wildly.

Leo stood quickly, knocking his chair over. He ran to the far end of the kitchen, grabbed the pitcher of water, and dashed back to my side. He pushed it into my hands and I began gulping directly from the lip. If Miss Celia saw me now, she would have a fit. Finally, the piece of bread dislodged from my throat and I could breathe again. I felt Leo's warm hands touching my neck as he held my hair.

"Are you all right?"

I nodded, feeling my face flush. "Thank you."

"Don't ever do that again. If I lost you to a measly bread crumb . . . " Leo let my hair fall and returned to his seat. "Not on my watch." He tapped the breast pocket of his uniform containing his watch.

"Yeah, I'll try to contain my choking habits to when you're off duty." *As if Leo O'Donnell was ever really off duty.* "I might as well tell you . . . " My voice trailed off, unsure of exactly how to explain it. "The fact is, Leo, that I am going away for a few weeks. It's a business affair of sorts." I didn't know what else to call it. "I can't go into much more detail. Miss Celia knows and has given her blessing. And you don't need to worry because Angela will be accompanying me."

Leo pressed his lips together looking as though he'd bitten a sour apple.

"I see, very well." Leo's face paled. "Please tell me, are you in some sort of trouble?"

"What? Nae, nae trouble at all!" I stammered to find the right words. Leo's sincerity made me feel guilty for not divulging every detail of the trip. The truth of the matter was that I didn't know all the details myself. *How could I explain what I was about to do since I was unsure myself?*

"This isn't much of my business, kid, but . . . does this sudden departure have to do with that Tree Man?"

Tremore. The utterance of his name made my hair stand on end.

"I can assure you that this has absolutely nothing to do with Tree Man." I laughed. "Apparently, you weren't informed that my cousin has left town for business purposes. I honestly don't suspect his return for a while." At least I hoped.

I reached across the table and squeezed Leo's hand.

"Good." Leo's shoulders relaxed as he tore another piece of bread. "You know, kid, I give you my word," that dimpled smile returned to Leo's face, "I'll make certain everything stays in tiptop shape around here."

CHAPTER 11

ANGELA AND I APPROACHED THE old bridge—the appointed place to meet with Albert Edward and Mr. Griffith. As promised, they were awaiting our arrival. When I walked across the bridge, I could hear the river rushing under toe.

"*Dia dhuit*, my lady," Jack greeted me, casually leaning against the stone arch. His oversized tweed jacket hung loosely around crossed arms, and his peaked cap pulled snugly over his head. He appeared so relaxed. I suppose adventure was nothing new to him. That was the life he lived by.

"Angela, I'm glad you'll be accompanying us." Albert Edward nodded towards Angela. It was refreshing to witness a man with proper dignity paying respects even to those society deem less fortunate. Then he turned his attention to me. "Did you sleep well, my lady?" Albert Edward kissed my hand.

"Are fairies real?" I joked.

Albert Edward let out a hard laugh. "I suppose that depends upon whom you ask. Let's hope that today is the day you believe."

"No such luck." Fairies were not real, to me. Likewise, I did not sleep well. I appreciated Albert Edward's jovial attitude, though, as it made me smile.

"Ah, well, that's to be suspected. Let us carry these things for you." First, he took the bag from my hand and passed it over to Jack. Then, he reached for the box containing Lover.

I gripped the handle, pulling her closer to my side. "Thank you, Albert Edward, but I can manage."

"Very well." Albert Edward began to walk, leading the way towards town. He turned back to me, carefully examining the case in my hand. "A fiddle, perhaps?"

I held my chin high. "Indeed. She has a special place in my heart. Although, it seems as of late that grief has kept me from playing, I thought . . . perhaps, if I brought Lover along she might be able to keep us in good company."

"Lover?" Albert Edward frowned.

"Oh, yes. Lover is her name. I know it's a bit absurd to name your fiddle, but she has special meaning, ya know."

"Brilliant. Absolutely brilliant!" Albert Edward's voice shrieked. "I'm delighted. A performance from the one and only Nora Gallagher was not what I'd expected."

I glanced at Jack and back to Albert Edward. "You realize that I'm not the only performer on this trip?"

Albert Edward cocked his head.

"Jack Griffith here is a master instrumentalist. My Pop hired him many times over the years, didn't he, Jack?" I gave Jack an encouraging nod. "You should know he's sought after to perform all over the county. I can't wait for you to hear him play."

"Surely the passing of time while we're on our voyage will be most enjoyable." Albert Edward responded by lifting his hands to the air in mild applause.

Jack tipped his hat in a wordless gesture of appreciation.

As we continued to walk, I wondered if the plan was to travel the distance by foot. "Where exactly are we headed?" I finally asked. I knew that our final destination was an island, a wee distance from the coast, but I didn't know how Albert Edward planned for us to travel.

"We're almost there." Albert Edward grinned as we followed him through town. The only sounds were our footsteps crunching beneath gravel and a family of crows cawing in cadence among the treetops. A thin ember peacefully streaked across the sky—daybreak was beckoning. At the edge of town, Albert Edward and Jack abruptly turned onto the boardwalk stretching toward the old pier behind the Trading Post. It was vacant.

At the end of the dock, a pristine yawl boat bobbed on top of the rippling current.

"Welcome aboard, my lady," Albert Edward announced.

I looked up at him wide-eyed. Having been on only a few small fishing excursions, I had never stepped foot on a rig of this magnitude.

"We're goin' fishing?" I was confused.

"Perhaps we'll sneak in some fishing, later." Albert Edward beamed. "Now, climb aboard . . . we haven't much time to lose if we want the tide to push us out to sea."

Sea? We were going out into the deep, open waters? This wasn't what I'd expected.

The boat was like-new and sparkling white, a pearly essence. On the side panel, painted in royal blue were the words, *An Saol Spiorad.*

I ran my hand over the raised letters. "Gaelic?" I'd studied the original Irish language and knew enough of the language to communicate, but these words, I didn't understand.

"Aye, 'The Spirit Lives'," Jack proclaimed.

That's an odd name for a yawl boat. Jack offered his hand to Angela and me as we hopped onto the boat.

"May I?" Jack extended his hand to Lover. "I'll put her in a safe place, my lady." I looked into Jack's worn eyes that seemed to whisper truth. Pop trusted Jack Griffith and so did I. I handed over our fiddle.

The ship was immaculate. It appeared as though it'd never been used. I suppose that shouldn't surprise me since Albert Edward's father was Lord Lieutenant. A scarlet sail hung loosely, flapping against the mast, and plush bench seats wrapped around the inside of the yawl.

My teeth were already chattering. It was probably nervousness but the biting wind did not help my jitters.

"Where is yer coat, my lady? You're gonna need it!" Albert Edward asked.

I shrugged off his instruction for a few moments until I could bear it no longer. I unclasped my bag and retrieved my red cloak. The frigid ocean air made me feel raw and exposed, and yet, I don't believe I'd ever felt so alive.

At first, the boat moved slowly, the water streaming along the backside of downtown Donegal Town. I glanced upon the embankment and saw the Abbey Hotel and the other shops and pubs stretched in a tight row. Everything familiar was rushing past me. Within moments, the unrelenting current pushed us beneath the old bridge's underpass and there, bursting forth in magnificent beauty, was Kings Castle perched upon the hill. My heart stilled. *I hope I'm making the right choice.*

Jack stood behind the enormous wheel navigating our way through the narrow canal. For a tinsmith by day and musician by night, he sure had a way with controlling this big vessel. It appeared as though he'd done this before—which, it was not unlike Jack to be seemingly equipped with an array of knowledge. Soon the river gave birth to the sea, and my view became vast and expansive like the sky above. It was breathtaking. Quite literally, the wind was taking my breath away. Angela took a seat on the bench encircling the yawl while I remained standing. I wanted to take in all the sights and sounds. The morning sun was effulgent and seemed to bounce off the ocean, glistening like diamonds. Once Jack steadied the boat, I watched as he effortlessly hoisted the sail and we began to sail smoothly into the Atlantic Ocean.

I couldn't help but keep looking back. The port from which we'd traveled was shrinking before my very eyes. The landscape appeared to be stretching further and further away too. *What if we got lost and couldn't find our way back! Were the hills dissolving before my very eyes?* I didn't want to worry, but my breath continued to come up short.

Albert Edward staggered to my side, hooking his arm with mine, I assumed for balance. "What seems to be the bother, my lady? You have a scowl upon your face."

"Ach! It's nothing." I twisted my body, looking again in the direction we'd just traveled.

"Do you want to go back?"

"Nae, not really." The sun was so bright I had to squint in order to see Albert Edward's face. "I suppose, if you must know, I'm a wee bit worried."

"Worried? Whatever for?"

I lifted my hand to my brow in an attempt to shade my view. "I'm not entirely sure. Lately it seems that I worry too much about making the wrong decisions. I never used to feel this way . . . not until my father died, anyway. Perhaps, this wasn't the best timing for me to leave the castle. Do you think?" I shrugged. "I mean, don't be fooled, I'm excited about an adventure. I've been aching to do this my whole life. Ya know, to get away and be free. It's just . . . I didn't imagine it would be like this."

"Tell me, my lady, what is it that you're most afraid of."

"Afraid of?"

"Aye, the thing that is causing you to look back." Albert Edward pointed to the distant coastline.

"Well, I told you already. I'm not certain that I should have left . . . and I suppose I fear that I won't be able to get back home."

"I see." Albert Edward lifted my hand and pressed it into his chest. "Nora Gallagher, you have my solemn promise that I shall rightfully return you to your home. This I swear." Albert Edward's playful smile and soft touch added a slight measure of comfort. He was an honest man. "Now, may I show you around?"

"Show me around?"

"You don't suppose I should have you sleep out in the elements, do you? I know yer a strong lady but that would take a great deal of gumption." Albert Edward laughed.

I steadied myself, still unaccustomed to the rocking movement of the ship. Jack grabbed my bag and followed us to the rear of the boat. A meager, square cabin extended from the base of the ship. Albert Edward opened the boxy door. There were a few steps leading to a room below and to the right a ladder extended to what appeared to be a similar room. "The men's quarters are above. You and Angela will reside down here." Albert Edward ducked as he escorted me into the quaint room. A bunk bed framed in polished wood was secured to the wall. Light poured into the dim chamber through one oval window.

"It certainly isn't a grand space—"

"It's perfect!" I looked around feeling content with the accommodations.

"I have an idea. Why don't you put your belongings away and lie down to rest for a bit? We'll be at sea for a few days now and I have a feeling you'll be needing your strength come tomorrow."

"Strength?"

"Our shipmate here, Jack Griffith, believes a storm is moving in." I felt my heart begin to pound beneath my chest. "Really?"

"But it's nothing we can't handle, my lady." Jack grinned.

When I woke, the cabin was dark. *How long had I been sleeping?* I peered out the window and saw the moonlight illuminating the ocean's waves and casting shadows upon the ship's vacant platform. I turned and saw that Angela was fast asleep in the top bunk. *It must be awfully late.*

As I stepped onto the deck, I noticed an awning had been secured to the cabin's outer wall stretching over an area of the ship's deck. The sides were flapping in the wind allowing me to notice that Jack was sitting alone with his back to me underneath this tent-like enclosure. Perhaps Albert Edward was asleep in his cabin? Jack's head bowed and I wondered if he, too, had fallen asleep. Lover was situated next to his feet. *Was Jack playing her while I was asleep?* As I attempted to return to my cabin so as to not disturb Jack, he swiftly lifted his head.

"Oh. Pardon me, Jack. I'm sorry to wake you."

"No bother, my lady. You didn't wake me." Jack's eyes shone like glass under the moon's reflection. "Come, sit over here." He pointed to a crate on the opposite side of the table.

"Are you hungry?" Jack uncovered a small platter containing a loaf of bread and stamp of butter.

I took a slice of bread, smearing it with butter.

"Shall we give thanks for this day?" Jack suggested, folding his hands.

I nodded and bowed my head.

"Dear Lord," Jack began praying, "May this food restore our strength, giving new energy to tired limbs and new thoughts to weary minds. May this drink restore our souls, giving new vision to dry spirits and new warmth to cold hearts. And once refreshed, may we give new pleasure to You, who gives us all. Amen."

Jack lifted his head. "Did you rest well?"

"I did, thank you. Is it the middle of the night?" I looked up at the stars on display overhead.

"It is. I guess you couldn't sleep neither?" Jack said. "I've been wonderin' . . . do ya have a favorite song?"

"A favorite song?" I considered the many ballads and reels I'd not only played but also danced to. I had many favorites. "It'd probably be something from Samuel Lover. Do you remember how much Pop loved his simple compositions?"

Jack responded with merely a flash of his winsome smile.

I continued, "*The Sunshine of The Heart*. I think it's one of Mr. Lover's most well-known pieces. I suppose, if I had to choose, this would be my favorite."

"Indeed, I've carried that tune before." Jack reached to pat the wooden box next to his foot. "I think it'd be fittin' to play a tune on the Gallagher family heirloom, aye?"

"Oh, yes! That's a grand idea." I bent down and picked up the box, placing it upon my lap. I lifted Lover from her box and gently handed her over to Jack.

"Would you do the honors?"

"Nora, I was thinking you ought to play. 'Tis why you brought Lover along. Isn't that so?"

I bowed my head at Jack's suggestion. I wanted to play again. In fact, I would play again; but the first time would be hard. The thought of playing without Pop's presence ever again broke my heart.

"I will. But the time isn't right, Jack. So, would *you* do the honors?"

"Very well then." Jack tucked Lover into the fold of his neck, placing his chin upon the rest. His eyes closed and I watched his fingers slide across the strings of her fingerboard. It was as if they were getting reacquainted. He seemed to hold her in a sweet embrace before placing the bow to her strings. The rich harmony began softly; soon Jack added his voice to the song:

The sunshine of the heart be mine
That beams a charm around;
Where'er it sheds its ray divine,
Is all enchanted ground!
. . . Beneath the splendour of thy ray
How lovely all is made!
. . . Sweet sunshine of the heart!

The song was sweet like honey, and I found it made my mind wander. *Now, why was I here on this boat?* I wiped the tears from my eyes, trying to recall the purpose for agreeing to come along with Albert Edward. For some reason, I was beginning to feel as though this call to adventure was more or less a quest to awaken from within.

CHAPTER 12

THE PIERCING SQUALL OF A bird jolted me from a deep sleep. It took me a brief moment to regain a sense of my surroundings. *Oh, I was still on the ship.* Raindrops had dried, leaving a speckled imprint upon the tiny cabin window. My body felt weak from exhaustion and I pulled the coverlet back over my head. After a few short moments, a tapping sound caused me to jerk my head from beneath my covers and I saw that a crow was perched outside my window, pecking at the glass, jilting its head back and forth, before flying away.

"Angela? Are you awake?" I whispered. When she didn't respond, I tiptoed out of bed and peeked at the top bunk. She was gone. Her covers were already neatly arranged for the day. I was surprised I didn't hear her moving about the cabin. I placed my bag onto my bed and shuffled through my belongings. In the process, I ran my hand across Mam's Bible and as I pulled it out, I felt my stomach growl. I was hungry, but something within was craving more than food for the day. It was a deep longing. Perhaps I desired for some kind of connection to Mam, or Pop, or maybe even God? I flipped through the pages of the Bible until I'd found those words in Isaiah that Mam underlined and I read them again.

"Though the mountains be shaken and the hills be removed,
yet my unfailing love for you will not be shaken

nor my covenant of peace be removed,"
says the Lord, who has compassion on you.

The cabin door flew open and Angela burst in. "I hoped you were awake! I came to assist you in preparing for the day. It's a blustery one, so you'll need to dress for the weather."

I looked again through the cabin window and noticed a low-lying haze clouded my view of the water.

"Is a storm coming?"

"The rain has moved past us. Mr. Griffith says he believes the clouds will part soon too. Who knows? We are at sea, after all, where the weather is as predictable as the potato crop."

Angela helped me select my clothes and pin my hair up for the day. Before I departed, she announced that she would stay back and tidy up the cabin, I suppose, to gain a reprieve from the elements.

When I emerged onto the platform, Jack was standing at the ship's wheel. Before I had a chance to fasten the buttons on my coat, a gust of wind lashed the deck of the yawl. I leaned against the cabin wall for support, securing the buttons on my coat as the ship swayed vigorously.

"It's bound to break soon," Jack hollered through the noise of thrashing wind. "Gonna be a mighty windy day though." Jack emphasized his words by pointing to the hoisted sail whipping through the current of wind. "Go, have a seat. Albert Edward will be with you shortly."

I stepped under the tent and found a slight relief from the chill. At least the violent gale was minimized. As I sat down, I observed a wooden platter covered with a silver dome placed in the center of the table. As I reached to lift the shiny lid, Albert Edward burst through the tent opening, interrupting my actions.

"On course!" He proclaimed as he sat beside me. "We may need to adjust the sail in a moment to keep us headed in the right direction though."

Hearing Albert Edward say that we were on course gave me a sense of hope. His jovial spirit awakened my senses and I said, "Despite the gloomy weather, someone appears to be in a fancy mood." I rubbed my hands together for warmth.

Albert Edward mimicked me by rubbing his hands together too. Then leaning forward, he uncovered the platter and revealed a heaping bowl of spiced currants and pine nuts, "Hungry?"

I nodded, reaching to scoop a spoonful of nuts. That's when another object on the tray caught my attention. It was a long tube, wrapped in royal blue satin, and tied on each end in white cords.

"What's this?" I asked, touching the silky fabric.

"Go on, open it."

Was this a gift, for me? I loosened the cinched ties and pulled off the satin. Inside I found a polished instrument. I twisted the unfamiliar object around in my hand and noticed one end was more narrow than the other. It was a viewer, I think—a fascinating kind of instrument I'd seen only in catalogs.

"'Tis a kaleidoscope," Albert Edward said excitedly. You might have thought he was the one receiving the gift.

"It's exquisite!" I said while still turning the object in my hand. Shiny brass hinges clasped the side of the tube and a lens of glass was fastened to the top and bottom of the cylinder.

"Do you know how it works?" he asked.

I peered through one end of the kaleidoscope and everything appeared distorted and blurry. "Not exactly."

"I can tell, you're looking at it through the wrong lens!" Albert Edward slapped his leg in amusement, and reaching for the instrument, he flipped it around for me. "There, now do you see?"

"Ach!" It was brilliant. A multitude of colors exploded in the most unusual pattern. It was like art: messy, scattered, and yet, oh so beautiful.

"Now, turn the kaleidoscope this way." Albert Edward's stubby fingers touched mine, prompting me to twist the device a certain way.

"Amazing!" Every time I twisted the tube, the image and colors completely transformed, displaying another unique design. I pulled my eye away from the lens, "This is the most beautiful gift!" I noticed Albert Edward looking at me curiously. "Where did you ever pick up such a fine present?"

"I guess you could say I'm a thief," he said.

I nearly choked on my pine nut. "What! You stole it?"

"Steal? Not entirely." I was concerned that the shrill of Albert Edward's laughter might cause the glass in my kaleidoscope to burst.

"Are you familiar with the tale of Robin Hood?"

"The childhood fable? Em, yeah. It was read to me often as a child."

"In essence, I like to conduct a similar affair."

"So, you're saying you take from the rich and give to the poor."

"Precisely." Albert Edward grinned, exposing his bright smile. I was somewhat taken aback.

"Oh." I didn't understand his point of view; I wasn't poor—why did he feel the need to give me something so extravagant? This sort of behavior made me question Albert Edward's true character. Perhaps, he wasn't the kind young man I'd deemed him to be? "So, you take a rich man's possession and turn around and give it to the poor?"

"It depends. Usually I trade it for cash first. Money tends to be more useful."

"But you've given me this beautiful gift and I don't need—"

"No, my lady. I apologize for any confusion. The kaleidoscope is not a gift for you. I st— rather collected—it from a landlord prior to our departure. Once we return, my personal merchant will trade it. I fully intend to use the proceeds to support the needs of the poor folks living on Moore Island," Albert Edward said.

Albert Edward's laughter was wild. Surely, it wasn't right to mislead folks, but I think I understood his appropriation. He was still helping the poor, even if it *was* in a roundabout way.

"Come now." Albert Edward stood, and, extending his hand to help me to my feet, he led me out from our enclosed space. A tiny patch of sunlight was attempting to break through the clouds.

"Take a look now."

I lifted the instrument toward the sky and looked again.

"Notice how the light changes everything," Albert Edward explained. He was right. The beauty I saw sitting beneath the tent was dismal in comparison to what I was seeing now.

I took a deep breath feeling a strange sense of peace come over me.

"Excuse me, Mr. Cooper," Jack ambled toward us. "I'm going to need your assistance controlling the wheel while I shift the sail."

I looked across the white-capped sea and wondered how he could control this yawl?

"Follow me," Albert Edward suggested.

"Remind me again, why we need to reset the sail?" I felt like I was hollering in his ear.

"Because our direction has shifted slightly and we need to account for the wind so that we hit our precise destination!"

"Oh." The motion of the waves made me feel dizzy. I watched Jack walk over and unwind the halyard, which loosed the sail. The yawl teetered even more wildly back and forth. I wrestled to hold my position as the force pulled us further out to sea. In a short time, I felt myself lean against Albert Edward for support. I looked up at Jack, desperately hoping he would hurry. I was feeling very insecure about this whole navigation thing. As I watched, Jack climbed the rungs of the mast and began pulling different ropes connected to the sail. I gasped at the sight. *What was he doing?* Despite the thrashing winds, he appeared to keep himself steady as he worked. No matter the condition, Jack Griffith made everything appear effortless. Within moments, the sail had been reset and the ship sailed onward at a steadier pace.

Standing on the deck I turned to Albert Edward and said, "Ya know, I was certain we'd be well on our way to Iceland by the way the ship was flailing about."

"Maybe on another adventure, my lady. But Iceland is not the island we're aimin' for today." Albert Edward pointed straight ahead. I squinted, but couldn't see anything except a pile of blotted colors way off in the distance. Was it a small mountain or simply a mirage? *There!* In the distance, a piece of land in muted sepia tones erupted from the sea. Was the tint of caramel from earth or sand? Were the shades of pewter a culmination of craggy rocks? The top of this island appeared to be covered in an array of green life. It looked almost like a small mountain without a peak.

"Moore Island," Albert Edward announced. The yawl's new alignment seemed to push us into an effortless glide closer to our destination.

CHAPTER 13

THE CLOSER WE CAME, THE smaller I felt compared to the breadth of this place. It took a little effort to maneuver *An Saol Spiorad* through the school of boulders erupting from the turbulent sea. Angela and I stood next to each other looking over the side of the boat and watched as the deep, blackcurrant waters swirled and twisted as if they were in agony. It caused me to wonder what sort of fish, if any, might be lurking below.

"All right, we're about to make landfall," Jack announced, gripping the wheel. "We should have enough momentum to push straight onto shore." The sand-swept beach stretched before my eyes as our vessel rushed the seaboard, splitting a line through the crystalized sand. Once the boat stopped, Jack hurried to drop the anchor.

"Well done, Mr. Griffith!" Albert Edward exclaimed. Walking towards the front of the yawl, he shielded his eyes to look up and down the coast. "Hmm . . . that's interesting."

"Is something wrong?" I, too, looked along the narrow seashore that was abruptly met by a steep embankment covered with shoots of various grasses, roots, and saplings.

"Typically, when I've conducted similar missions, the village folks will begin to crowd upon arrival. This is unusual."

"Oh. So what should we do?"

"We'll go find them." Albert Edward turned to face me. "I should warn you, a painful scene likely awaits us, but first, do you want to fish?"

"Huh?" I shook my head. Albert Edward's shift confused me. "I thought we had work to do."

"When we started out on this voyage you asked if we would go fishing. So?" Albert Edward lifted his chin towards the sky. "It appears the storm is past us."

"But our focus is to assess the needs of these islanders."

"Aye, the mission remains the same," he said. Walking over to the bench, he lifted the seat, revealing a small space for storage, and retrieved the fishing poles and a basket from the hidden compartment. "Except, I realized last night that it might be proper to introduce ourselves bearing a proper gift, something of nourishment. I mean, look around. It's desolate."

"You mean, a basket of fish?" I interjected.

"Indeed, my lady!"

"Where do you suppose is the best place to catch fish?" When I was a child, Pop had often taken me fishing down by the river, but sea fishing was going to be different, I suppose. I looked across the shoreline. On one end, I saw an enormous boulder nearly leaning into the ocean. The waves lapped against the stone as though it were a thirsty dog finally getting a drink. On the hillside, above the boulder, a groove carved in the landscape created a slight ravine. I guessed it probably slid down the hill eons ago, leaving its imprint on the world.

Jack lifted his head, turning to look across both angles of the seaboard. "We should each find a different nook to fish from." He pointed to a few visible spots tucked among the rocks and sea.

Angela tugged on my elbow and whispered, "If it's all right with you, I'd prefer to maintain things here on the ship."

"Very well, if you wish." I brushed my arm around her shoulder, giving her a little hug. Angela had been pretty quiet, thus far. I'm sure being away from John was on her mind.

Jack prepared the fishing lines for Albert Edward, himself, and me. Each of us took a rod and dispersed to find our own spot. I walked a distance in the direction of the boulder. As I approached the area, I noticed a stream trickling through a crevice of the rustic terrain. I climbed over the mangled rock formations strewn about the shore and discovered a cove, inset from the thrashing waves—a place where the deep, placid water appeared as if it would be ideal for casting my rod.

I sat down on a small rock and began casting my line. I leaned back, peering along the shoreline. At a distance, I could see both Jack and Albert Edward with their rods attempting to catch fish. *An Saol Spiorad* was secured to the coastline, bobbing from the ebb and flow of the water. It was good to be alone with my thoughts and I was reminded of all the fond memories I had as a child with my Pop. There was something about the act of fishing that evoked a feeling of being free. Perhaps it was the simplicity. As I watched the thin, meandering line from my pole submerge, it brought on unexpected feelings of delight. My pole jerked as the line disappeared into the water. I reeled with all my strength until a speckled Coalfish emerged from the deep.

As I placed the catch in my basket, I heard a rustling behind me. I spun around, releasing the pole to the ground. At the very top of the hill, the grass was swaying. *Was it the wind?* I couldn't tell because my cove was isolated from the elements. I thought I was alone. My heart pulsed as I surveyed the hillside; all I could see was craggy rock and wild vegetation. The tall grass continued to move, but still, I saw no one. *Was it an animal?* I'm sure it was nothing, but I couldn't contain my curiosity. I scooped up my pole and basket of fish, wondering the best route to hike. The incline was severe and I had to steady myself after each rigorous step. I stopped partway to catch my breath. Now that I was higher up, I could see so much more of the landscape. The wide-open sea was a picturesque backdrop; it seemed as if it belonged on canvas in a famous art gallery. Looking around me, I studied the plants and bushes that bore in the ground and suddenly, there, hunkered down amidst a patch of turf was a small boy. I blinked hard. *Was this real?* I couldn't believe it. The boy's body formed a ball as he attempted to hide in the brush. His long, boney fingers covered his face, his desperate attempt to remain unseen. But from where I stood, he was easy to see. I stepped cautiously toward him. I kept a short distance and observed his unusual behavior for several moments. His hair was slick like an oil rag. He was very young, but the lines on his weathered face made him appear aged. I set down my belongings, pulled up my skirt, and knelt down to his level. Then, the boy slightly lowered his hand and slowly opened his eyes. He sat completely still and stared past me as if I were invisible. As he blinked, I noticed his dreamy eyes were the color of a fawn. Looking at him made me feel a bit uneasy, but something about him mysteriously drew me in.

I looked down toward the shore. Both Albert Edward and Jack were looking up at me. We were too far of a distance for me to shout so I waved for them to come.

Shifting my attention to the boy I muttered, "Hello, boy. What's your name?"

The boy cinched his eyes closed.

I scooted a wee bit closer to him, noticing the way his bedraggled muslin shirt sagged to expose his emaciated shoulders. He did not look well.

"Where are your parents?" I asked.

The boy's straight-faced expression made me wonder if he understood what I was saying. Behind me, I heard the sounds of heavy breathing as Albert Edward and Mr. Griffith labored to walk up the steep hill. As they approached, I pointed to the boy still hidden in the grass and shrugged. Then the boy stood, taking me by surprise, and reached to hold my hand. I stood up too, grabbing my belongings with my other hand. He tugged and I followed, with the men closely in tow. I noticed the boy wasn't wearing any shoes and his feet were calloused and dirty. As we reached the top of the hill, the ground plateaued.

The boy pointed across the bumpy green field; along the farthest edge, a dense black fog plumed into the air. As we ambled along, no one spoke a word. Reaching the border of the long field, the four of us stood in a line and peeked over the ridge. To our discovery, an entire village sprawled across the slope. Stone huts made of mud and thatch dotted the west-facing coast; some were partially erect and some were nearly falling over. Men, women, and children sat on rocks and stumps outside their homes. At first glance, it appeared as though it was a lazy day and folks were simply taking a moment to bask in the rare sun. Except, I quickly realized that this was not the case. This was the most eerie place I'd ever seen. A death-like stillness hovered over the village giving me the worst feeling of desperation. A man with a long stick standing near the smoldering fire noticed our arrival. As he walked over to greet us, Albert Edward stepped forward.

"Is this your father?" I whispered to the boy.

Without answering, the boy abruptly let go of my hand and walked away.

This man approached. "*Dia dhuit*," he said as he politely tipped his head. "Anthony *is ainm dom*." The man was introducing himself to us in Irish.

"My name is Albert Edward Cooper," Albert Edward announced. "And this is Lady Nora Gallagher and our shipmate Mr. Jack Griffith." I curtseyed, as my name was given, as I had been trained to do.

"Are you lost?" Anthony probed, communicating to us in our own language.

"Nae, not lost. We sailed in this morning. We've been sent on a mission from the Mansion House Relief Committee to access your needs. It's been reported to our Dublin headquarters that you may or may not be in need of"—Albert Edward's head twisted around scanning the ground around us as if he'd dropped a small coin—"some assistance."

Anthony let out a slight laugh, causing the other villagers to smile and laugh.

"Please explain what you mean by way of 'some assistance,' Mr. Cooper, because if you're referring to that rancid Indian meal being shipped over as an effort to alleviate our present starvation, you should know it's done more harm than good." Anthony took his stick and pointed to the very bottom of the slope where mounds of turf had been dug up and replaced by a mountain of stones. "We've lost hundreds."

I stared at the sight of it. *No, it couldn't be.* Those weren't stones, they were bones, and that desecrated bone yard ravine hardly satisfied a dignified burial site.

"I'm sorry, I was not made aware of these troubles. I suppose that is why we've been sent. Our hope is to provide a report to the committee of your specific needs and have those items distributed upon our immediate return." Albert Edward turned towards me, waving me to his side. I stepped forward and Albert Edward said, "I know it's not much, but would you kindly accept this basket of fish on our behalf?"

I leaned forward, extending the basket to Anthony.

He peered into the basket and upon seeing the caught fish, he fell to his knees and exclaimed, "Today we must celebrate!" Anthony raised his arms in the air worshipfully. Turning to the others he exclaimed, *"ní mór dúinn a cheiliúradh*!"

I watched as the villagers became elated. A few women clapped, and the children screamed with delight as they began chasing each other in circles. The boy, however, remained quiet.

Albert Edward's brow lifted with a look of astonishment. "A celebration? I'm sorry but I think you may have—"

"Aye, a celebration! You are our guests and for that we are grateful. Today is a special day!" Anthony began walking around and shouting instructions to some of the villagers. "We shall prepare our best meal for you!"

I started to shake my head in defiance. How could they possibly propose to treat me to their finest meal? It felt wrong to accept. I said, "Mr. Cooper, tell them no. They can't do this for us. They can't even provide for themselves!"

"I know, Nora. I've seen this before. But we cannot deny them this. It is who they are and it would be a huge disgrace if we don't accept their offer. It's hard to look upon the face of suffering, but you must remember we are here to help."

I nodded. I suppose Albert Edward was right. How could we possibly say no? I looked at the people shuffling around, excited and hurried as if a match had been struck to light their way.

When Anthony returned from giving out instructions, I asked him, "Can you tell me about the boy?" I gently touched the boy's arm causing him to look up at me.

"The boy is dumb. He cannot speak," Anthony said.

"Are you his father?"

Anthony smiled, but shook his head. "The boy is an orphan."

"Oh." I bit down, forcing my mouth to stay closed. He was so young to be without parents. I looked at the boy and my insides ached for him. No wonder he appeared distressed as if he carried a load of peat on his back. I swallowed hard because I understood the agony associated with suddenly becoming a fatherless child.

"What's his name?"

"His name is George." Anthony beamed as he patted the top of the boy's head. "He lives with me and my family," he said, pointing to a whitewashed cottage. "Although, we all take care of him, as well as the other children without parents. We consider ourselves one family."

A tear streaked my cheek and I quickly swiped it away.

"George finds enjoyment near the water. Most often we'll find him sitting upon the ridge or perched along the shoreline. I think he's drawn to the sound. He has a keen ear, that one."

"Aye, that's precisely where I discovered him, or rather, where he found me!" I laughed.

I felt a tap upon my shoulder and turned to see Jack standing at my side.

"Excuse me, my lady, but if the boy here is keen to sound, perhaps I could go fetch Lover for you. I mean, a celebration wouldn't be a celebration without music, would it?"

"Well, Mr. Griffith, I don't know." I gave Albert Edward and Anthony a quick glance. "I suppose that is a grand way to celebrate. Very well, if you don't mind, go on and fetch Lover. And while you're there, please tell Angela to come and join us. This is an event she should experience."

As Jack tipped his hat and turned to depart for the yawl, George stepped forward and grabbed a hold of my fingers.

I bent over, to meet the boy face to face, and in response, he squinted his eyes shut. In an attempt to earn his trust, I said, *"Dia dhuit,* George. Nora, *is ainm dom."*

His brilliant blue eyes opened wide at this and his mouth puckered in delight as if he'd been given something sweet. George squeezed my fingers tighter and proceeded to pull me in the direction of the village.

By now, most of the villagers had assembled around the fire, watching closely as George and I approached. Typically this would make me feel as though I should run and hide. The fear of being scrutinized often gave my skin a crawling sensation, this, however, felt different. I sensed by the way they smiled that their stares were out of genuine curiosity, and I felt strangely at peace with it.

Anthony came up from behind us and began speaking to his people in Irish. In my mind, I unscrambled his words as best as I could: *Good day brothers and sisters. We have some new friends, Lady Nora Gallagher and Mr. Albert Edward Cooper.*

The villagers grinned, some toothless, and others poked at each other. I curtseyed, in awe at the notion that they would call me friend when we'd just met. At my side, George seemed to grow a little taller as if he'd just discovered a new toy.

A woman, bent over at the waist, wormed her way forward. Her faded dress was torn and cowling at the neck. *"Gabhaimid buíochas le Dia do shon."*

"We thank God for you." Anthony relayed the distraught woman's greeting.

"Maeve *is ainm dom.*" Her eyes swirled as though they were searching for a soft place to rest.

"Thank you for your kindness," I replied, but I had to look away for fear I would stare at the ridged lines protruding from her collar.

"Come," Anthony said, pointing in the direction of his cottage.

As we entered the dark, smoky, floorless abode, I noticed a bed of thatch was pressed along the corner wall. Where were the hens or the livestock, I wondered? In the center of the room a pile of ash lay heaped upon the floor, releasing the pungent aroma of peat and causing my nose to twitch.

Albert Edward folded his arms and stood a little taller. "I've been informed that your people have maintained a good moral character and as of late, been quite industrious or self sufficient. Forgive me, but since our arrival I've yet to notice any animal roaming about the island. Can you explain?" He coughed.

Anthony bowed his head. "For many years our small island has suffered great losses. First, the great famine—almost forty years ago—nearly destroyed us. We lost mothers, brothers, uncles, and children, and yet many survived. In time, we were able to replenish our supply of cows for milk, sheep for wool, geese for beds and hens with eggs. We began to grow our oats, barley, and potatoes again and were doing great . . . until the potato disease returned. At first, we managed, until eventually we ate our fowls, then our sheep, and now the cows. We have nothing left except the fish in the sea and the turf in the ground. There has been little to do to halt the desolation."

"I see." Albert Edward gripped his arms tighter than before. He had warned me we might encounter a painful scene. "We give you our word," Albert Edward snapped a look in my direction, "we will do whatever it takes to bring relief to your people." At this, Albert Edward's coughing resumed until he nearly doubled over. "Excuse me—" He ducked beneath the doorway of the cottage, and I followed suit.

Outside, the islanders stood in a circle around the cauldron, which was resting upon burning embers. The smell of boiled fish comingled with the array of stench I'd already been subjected upon was cause for my stomach to lurch. As I looked around at the group of people, I saw that Jack had returned from the yawl with Lover in his hand, and Angela by his side. Albert Edward and I joined them.

"'Tis a grand evening. Let us partake in this bounty," Anthony announced.

We were invited to sit on wooden stools around the fire as we enjoyed the sparse supply of food. Once we finished, I noticed something peculiar come over Albert Edward. He appeared distraught so I asked, "Is something bothering you?"

He held his hand to his chest. "I must be coming down with a cold. My insides feel as though they're burning up. Perhaps, I need to lie down."

"Very well. We'd best be going anyway. The longer we delay our return, the worse off these poor folk will be." I stood, tucking my arm into Albert Edward's. As he tried to stand, I felt him lean into me for support. Oh. Perhaps he really was coming down with something.

George rushed to my side; his knowing eyes begged a sadness I'd never before seen in a human being.

"The boy has taken to you, my lady," Anthony said.

"Ach! It pains me to have to leave him, to leave all of you . . . " I felt something slip into my free hand and I looked down to see Jack's hand pushing Lover into mine. I grabbed hold of Lover, unsure what to do, until I looked up and saw Jack wink in approval.

"Who, me? I thought you'd do the honors."

"Not tonight, Lady Nora. Make this your parting gift to these fine people."

I looked at Albert Edward who'd begun shivering, "But, Albert Edward's coming down with—"

"Let me escort him to the ship. I'll return for you and Angela. Very well?"

I nodded. Turning back towards the villagers and taking Lover from her case, I held her up and said, "May I?"

Their mild applause quickly followed with a supreme stillness as I returned to my wooden stool. George collapsed to his knees, sitting by my feet.

I placed Lover beneath my chin and a feeling of renewal came over me. I hadn't played since that fateful day. Today was fateful in its own right. No one deserves the kind of suffering that these God-fearing folks have had to endure, but I sensed deep down that something good would come of it. Before we came there was little hope, but now, because of a simple promise, these people would have something to hang onto. I lifted my head and began to turn the bow up and across the strings. The melody seemed to join the curling smoke streams, lifting toward the sky in a cadence of its own. I played a few songs, including the latest hymn that Jack had taught me. I secretly wished I had a way to capture the look of amusement upon George's face. It was as I'd suspected, the boy had an ear, all right. Knowing his story made me yearn to hold him, to spend time teaching him things like how to play the fiddle. Perhaps, one day I would brave the elements and journey back to Moore Island.

When it was time to leave, a few of the villagers, including George, escorted Angela and me to the ridge overlooking *An Saol Spiorad* because Jack hadn't returned for us. I brushed away tears as we said our good-byes. It was strange how, in such a short span of time, your life's perspective could change so dramatically.

CHAPTER 14

BENEATH THE DOORWAY, A BEAM of sunlight penetrated the drab Trading Post's storage room floor. The crate I sat on creaked as I shifted my weight to lean against the wall. Muffled voices beat against my back as Angela and John's worried conversation seemed to hum with the configuration of small talk and making trade. Details surrounding our return trip home seemed fuzzy in my mind, but I did recall Albert Edward becoming dreadfully sick with fever on the way. *How had we managed to survive?*

As the door burst open, daylight swarmed into the dark room like a colony of bees, and my weary body jolted. My vision blurred and I tried to distinguish the elongated figure coming towards me. A man entered alone. I squinted, slowly regaining my sight. *Was he wearing a uniform?*

"Leo?" *At last.* Thank goodness John had been at the Trading Post when we first arrived. The timing couldn't have been more perfect. Upon seeing Albert Edward's condition, John called for a doctor and transport to his home. Then he ushered Angela and myself into the Trading Post. I said I'd wait in the storage room until Leo arrived to take me to the castle. I combed my fingers through my tangled hair as I tried to stand, but my sea legs tossed me to the side.

"I'm here, now." Leo hooked his arm around my waist and swept me upright. "What happened to you, kid?" His strong hands gripped my shoulders, gently guiding me back down to a seated position. "Are you injured?"

"I'll be all right—I'm only a wee bit shaken," I stammered, shaking my head. How could I explain everything that happened on the voyage? George's innocent face, milky brown eyes, and the tears that streaked his cheeks when I departed kept replaying in my mind. "I've returned. That's all that matters." Perhaps I would tell him in due time, but not now.

"I've never seen you in such a . . . " he mumbled under his breath. Then, he spun around and began rummaging through the shelves. What was he looking for? He climbed the merchant's ladder to the highest shelf, fumbled through an open crate, and pulled out a wool blanket.

"You've never seen—what?" I looked down at my filthy dress, instantly understanding Leo's concern. My hem was frayed clear up to my ankles—I doubted even Angela could repair it—and my boots were untied and the sleeves of my blouse were stained with dirt. If I was privy to a mirror, I'm certain my face and hair would mimic the rest of my appearance. *What a disheveled mess!*

"I think you should see a doctor!" Leo wrapped the blanket around my trembling body.

"Nae, I'm not hurt. I just need rest. Please take me home, I think I shall sleep for five days through."

Leo squinted his eyes with a concerning look. I'd seen that look before: the way he calculated before a mission. "There's one thing you ought—" he hesitated.

"Leo, can we please discuss this later? I'm not in the frame of mind to think or speak rationally." My mind was too weary to engage in any serious conversation.

Without warning, Leo scooped me up and began to carry me outside, across the boardwalk, and toward the jaunting car.

"Wait! My belongings. They're still in the ship."

"John has already retrieved your things. He and Angela have taken care of the items on the boat." *What a relief.* I felt my body sink into Leo's embrace. If I were in the right frame of mind, I'd demand that Leo set me down. What if other townsfolk saw me in this state? But I simply didn't have the strength to argue—I was too weak to even walk! So I buried my head and prayed no one would see us.

"Well, well, well . . . is that really you, Nora Gallagher?"

Leo's muscles flinched. I could pin that high-pitched, squeaky voice anywhere. Violet Ellison, the town gossip . . . and my least favorite person. I strained to lift my head and surely, it was her. My prayer was too little, too late.

"It's okay, Leo. Set me down so I can walk," I said. Leo's face paled. *Was something bothering him?*

"Good day, Violet." I attempted to walk in a straight line, but my wobbly legs caused me to swerve like someone who'd overindulged at the pub. Leo hooked his arm into mine, preventing my collision with a hitching post.

"It appears you've endured quite the hardship during your recent expedition, if ya don't mind me sayin'." Violet scrunched her nose as she looked me up and down.

"How do you suppose?" I patted my untamed hair.

"Perhaps that dear, old servant woman . . . what's her name again? Oh yeah, Miss Celia! Perhaps, next time you travel, you could invite her along? Ahem . . . you know, someone like yourself can never have too much assistance these days." Violet's mouth formed a stiff grin.

I was beginning to feel warm. If I wasn't so tired, I might have done something awful to remove that hideous look from her face. Then we'd see who was really in need of assistance.

"My care was greatly attended to and the voyage was grand! Thank you for inquiring, Violet. Good day!" What she didn't know was that Angela and I had cared night and day for poor, sick Albert Edward. I looked up at Leo, pleading with my eyes that he get me away from this catty woman. Leo swiftly guided me to the passenger's seat.

"Hello, Leo." Violet fanned herself. "Ain't you a sight for sore eyes."

"Good day, Violet." Leo politely nodded, then brushed my arm. "Are you all set, my lady?"

"More than you know."

Leo climbed to his seat, snapped the reigns, and didn't look back.

"Pay no mind to Violet Ellison," Leo said. Was he trying to convince himself too? By the looks of his ridged disposition, I sensed he was trying to shake off the encounter. Clearly, her effect lingered.

"Do you still love her?" My curiosity got the best of me.

"Excuse me . . .?"

"Violet. You courted her, aye? Didn't you go so far as asking her Da—"

"With all due respect, it's water under the bridge." He lifted his chin. "Besides, we've more important things to set our minds upon!"

Of course he still loved her. Angela had told me the whole story. He wanted to make Violet his bride until her father condemned the relationship, saying Leo didn't have the means to take his daughter's hand. Leo had been crushed. Perhaps this was his motivation behind his hard work at the castle? My mouth dropped at the realization. I'd always wondered why he was so bent on proving his worth. Was this his effort to boost his confidence and self-worth? Or was he still trying to win Violet over?

As we came round the bend, approaching the old bridge, Leo pointed toward the castle. "I know you don't want to hear it, but you ought to know . . . " Leo hesitated. "He showed up last night."

"Pardon?"

"Tremore is back."

Perhaps Violet Ellison wasn't my least favorite person after all.

Despite sleeping in my own bed for the first time in days, the quality of rest was partial. There were simply too many things churning in my mind. *How would Tremore treat me since our last encounter? Which requests should I respond too? Was attending the Herbert School of Music something I should contend with? What could I do to help George and my new island friends?* Eventually, I succumbed to my restlessness and decided to get ready for the day. I slipped into my striped day dress with the pleated ruffle capping my shoulders. I stood before my mirror while buttoning the standing collar. It wasn't my favorite ensemble, but at least I was clean since thankfully, Miss Celia had poured a hot bath for me upon my return last night. I ran a brush through my washed hair before tucking a floral comb in place for added measure.

In the great room, I took a seat at the table to await Miss Pavek's arrival with my tea. I picked up the copy of *The Examiner,* placed on the edge of the table, and nearly fell out of my seat when I read the headline, *Castle's Fair Day Program Failing.*

As I began to frantically read the column, I felt Miss Pavek's hand brush against mine. She set a tray in front of me filled with scones, jam, and tea.

"'Tis a shame." She spoke in hushed tones.

I set the paper down and looked up at her. "You know about this?"

"I read the account this morning, no sooner than you, my lady," Miss Pavek said.

"I don't understand. Why hasn't this matter been brought to my attention?" I picked up my cup and sipped my tea. "I mean, the Fair Day program was one of my father's . . . I had no idea that it was failing!"

Miss Pavek stood quietly, shaking her head.

"How do you do this fine morning, my lady?" O'Riley announced as he bound through the kitchen door.

"O'Riley! You're just the person I need to speak with." I jumped from my chair and pressed the newspaper into his chest.

"Likewise," he said, crinkling the paper in his fist. "I hope your travels were well suited, yes?"

I straightened my shoulders and returned to my seat. I needed to get control of myself.

"Indeed. My journey was quite, well, rather adventurous." I reached for a scone, still warm from the oven. I tore it in half and the rich smell of pastry and butter stirred my hunger. The smell of home was helping to calm my nerves. I took a deep breath and continued, "Do you know what this story is all about?"

O'Riley pierced his lips together. Tossing the paper onto the table, he took a seat across from me. "There is a logical explanation. You see, in the aftermath of your father's death, we had to make some immediate changes. Initially, when the successor was still unknown . . . " O'Riley cleared his throat. "I took it upon myself to modify the Fair Day program until further notice."

"What? Why would you do that? This was important to my father."

O'Riley raised an eyebrow.

"Listen, my lady, we are all reeling from the loss of your Pop!" O'Riley's voice cracked. "I don't expect you to understand the bond I had with your father. Nonetheless, this was not an easy decision. We're all tired and strained from the extra effort it's taken to bring justice to your father's name. You don't understand that our economy is in a state of crisis. I've learned a few tactics over the years and the best way to manage a fractured structure is to stop the overflow. So that's what I did, I halted the excess spending. I certainly hope you can trust me. I really do know what's best for the castle." The corner of O'Riley's mouth turned up.

I wanted to understand his opinion but it didn't add up. Even though we were a weakened people, distraught with grief, why should that stop us from doing good?

"Can I be honest, my lady?" O'Riley continued before I could reply. "The castle, our servants, the community—our entire economy—is at a loss without a prominent leader." He stood from his chair, "I believe it would be wise to seriously consider Tremore's proposal."

Ach! Tremore? Did O'Riley really find this to be a valid suggestion? Because I didn't.

"He is a strong businessman with an understanding of how this castle operates. Despite his rough attitude at times, I'm confident that the legacy of Kings Castle is of utmost priority to him."

I scratched at my collar, beginning to feel overheated. "What does that man know about my legacy? Nothing!" I shouted before I had a chance to think about a more appropriate way to respond.

"My lady, there are times in life when you have to look beyond yourself. It's about choosing what is best for the welfare of all the people. I know it's hard to hear, but in my opinion, the castle should be administered by someone with experience. Someone with gumption. Someone who will fight to stand against the forces that be."

"Gumption? Fight to take a stand? I see."

O'Riley continued, "With all due respect, if you don't choose a suitor soon, you'll risk losing your inheritance to Tremore, anyway. My advice is to accept—"

At that moment, the kitchen door swung open and Tremore stepped into the room. He wore a dark, pressed suit and his hair was combed back. The red handkerchief fanning from the pocket near his lapel accentuated his dapper way with the latest Victorian trends. In fact, I imagined he'd make a perfect model for the Charles Worth pamphlet. His cologne, wafting into the air, overpowered my train of thought. There was no denying that Tremore Gallagher was handsome, but I hated the way his presence demanded my attention.

"Ahh, 'tis a pleasure to see you, Nora. I trust your venture was to your satisfaction." Tremore walked up to me, reaching for my hand.

Fighting against my will, I responded dutifully and lifted my hand. Tremore held it for a long awkward moment before pressing his cool lips onto my skin.

"Indeed, it was life-changing." I stood up, feeling as though I was no longer hungry. "I'll admit, I'm a bit surprised to see you back . . . so soon."

The two men gave each other an uncertain look.

"I was about to tell Lady Nora about the meeting," O'Riley changed the subject.

"Very good, I'll escort you to the quarters." Tremore fixed his gaze upon me.

"Meeting?" I questioned.

"Yes, that was what I wanted to advise you of." O'Riley shuffled his feet as if he were suddenly plagued with discomfort. "We're holding a meeting at the gatehouse to discuss future plans for Kings Castle. You're welcome to join us, if you wish."

"I'm glad you've come around to mentioning it, O'Riley." My words were coming out sharply, but I couldn't help it. "I'll be there," I snapped, "Because the future affects us all—the whole economy."

My head was throbbing. I wanted to escape, to run away, even if it were just up the stairs and into the comfort of my bed. But then I remembered, reprieve wasn't what I needed. What I needed was to see things from a different perspective, to understand that there is more than meets the eye when it comes to our circumstances or trials.

I showed up at the gatehouse for the pre-arranged meeting. The servants stood in small circles conversing. Tremore, John, Frank, and Leo were present too.

O'Riley called the meeting to order. "I'm sure many of you have read today's front page article in *The Examiner*." He waved a copy of the paper in the air. "A short time ago, I made the grievous decision to halt the Fair Day program because of the financial demands placed upon us during this season of mourning."

Several men bobbed their heads in silent agreement.

"I know this year has been hard. Life-changing for all of us. But we must not allow our sorrows to consume our duty. In the future, we may consider bringing the program back, but that timing is uncertain."

From my spot in the back of the room, I could see Leo stood a head taller than most of the other men. I looked around the room to observe who was present and when my gaze turned back to Leo, I caught him staring at me. I wondered why he was glaring at me, but he kept staring at me until I had to look away.

O'Riley reached for a piece of paper from his desk and began discussing a number of items he'd written down: things like the town's railway expansion and taking extra care to maintain the grounds for when prospective suitors visited. Perhaps my body was still lagging from my travels, but as O'Riley spoke, I couldn't concentrate on his words.

After everyone dispersed from the meeting, Leo caught up to me in the courtyard.

"Well done, kid."

"What are you talking about, Leo? I didn't do anything."

"That's not the way I see it. You were present, weren't you?"

"I . . . em, I suppose."

"Whether you realize it or not, that makes a statement."

"Yeah, I don't know—" I continued to stomp towards the castle. "I ought to trust, right?" I laughed to keep from crying.

Leo grabbed my arm and whispered, "I don't think you're gonna find this funny." The centers of his eyes were dark. He gripped my arm tighter and began to pick up the pace until we rounded the side of the castle, near the pantry door.

"Leo? You're scaring me."

He opened the jacket of his uniform, exposing a long, hard, covered book.

"I want you to take this, go straight to your keep and find a safe place to review it. Keep it hidden until we get this figured out, do you hear me? I've discovered something you need to be aware of."

"What is this?"

"'Tis your father's financial ledger."

CHAPTER 15

LEO WAS RIGHT; THE FINANCIAL ledger was no laughing matter. It took me a time to figure out the system for recording transactions. The recording of various tenant's rental income compared to the ongoing list of expenses was quite extensive. Upon further review, it became increasingly clear that something was amiss. Our financial picture appeared more dire than I expected. It was odd; the income column showed regular deposits and nothing looked out of the ordinary in the expense column. But when I saw the Fair Day dole crossed out in the ledger, I was puzzled. It was strange. Shouldn't the bottom line prove positive once the Fair Day expense was removed? But it did not; rather, it continued at a steady decline. How? I ran my finger down the description of payees and stopped at one name in the ledger that left me scratching my head.

T.G. Musical Academy

The very day the Fair Day allotment was canceled, this unusual expense was penned in. It was repeated a few more times thereafter. Hmm. I couldn't remember the last time I'd received a proper music lesson. *What was T.G. Musical Academy and why were they receiving a sizable contribution from the castle?* I'd never heard of such a place. Perhaps Pop hired someone on his own time? But wait . . . I traced my finger across the ledger; the date of issuance was after Pop's death.

T.G. Musical Academy. I strained to place the name.

T.G.

T . . . T . . .

I gasped. It couldn't . . . he wouldn't . . . Tremore?

Tremore Gallagher Musical Academy.

How could—or better yet, *why* would—Tremore be receiving payments from the castle? A closer look revealed that O'Riley signed each payment.

I felt cheated. Another heart-wrenching blow. I knelt at the foot of my bed and wept. It was too much to bear. *Why me, God? Why do these horrible things keep happening to me?*

I felt a surge of anger and beat my fists against my bed. I wanted to stomp the floorboards like a child. My throat became thick and swollen. I choked for breath and my tears soaked my blouse as I wept until I had nothing left in me. Eventually, the wailing gave way to a mind-throbbing hum and a sense of longing shivered throughout my body.

I walked over to my window, my spirit feeling taxed. I looked out and observed what appeared like a watercolor portrait of the Bluestack Mountains. Instantly, I felt the words I'd read from Mam's Bible wash over me.

"Though the mountains be shaken and the hills be removed,
yet my unfailing love for you will not be shaken
nor my covenant of peace be removed,"
says the Lord who has compassion on you.

I suddenly realized that this verse wasn't referring to the mountains actually being removed. It was a symbol for all the big, beautiful things in my life. What God was telling me was that no matter what comes and goes, the mountains or the hills, the big and the small, His love would never depart and His promise of peace would stay with me forever.

I bowed my head, surrendering to this humble realization. "Oh Lord, give me wisdom to see things Your way."

Albert Edward was on the mend, and thankfully it wasn't the dreaded "famine fever" that the doctor had been concerned about. His footman had sent word that after a few days' rest and much needed hydration, Albert Edward was feeling better. I responded by extending an invitation to the castle for dinner, so today, beauty treatments were in order.

After knocking, Angela poked her head into my chamber, "I thought I'd come before the others arrive." She stepped into my room and closed the door behind her. "How are you feeling?"

I rushed to embrace her. "Oh. I'm recovering from the turbulent sea just fine. It's the turbulent Tremore and, dare I say, O'Riley that are causing the aches and pains." The company of my dear friend brought me a great deal of comfort.

"You have no idea how grateful I am that we're home, safe and in one piece. I was quite worried the entire time we were away. I missed John terribly." Angela crossed my room, placing her bag on the floor, near my desk. "'Tis a good thing we returned when we did. John went and burned up every last candle in our possession. I'll be sewing patches on his knees for weeks with all the prayin' he did for us while we were away." Angela grinned, even though I suspected she was being quite honest.

I scooted toward my desk, curious to see what ensemble might be tucked away in Angela's bag. Noticing the letters I'd sorted in my letterbox, I pulled the top three envelopes from the pile so that I remembered to give them to Miss Celia when she arrived.

Angela overtly stared at the letters in my hand.

"I'm simply obliging Miss Celia." I answered the question Angela so clearly had written across her creased forehead.

Angela slouched as she fumbled through her bag. "How goes the task?"

I sighed. "I'd rather be doing more important things."

Angela lifted several garments from her bag and began spreading them in a neat display upon my bed. A solemn look tugged at the corners of her mouth and she looked as though she might cry.

"Is everything all right?" I asked.

She lifted her head and gave me a look of desperation. "Well, I guess if ya don't mind me sayin' it straight out . . . "

Angela always spoke plainly with me—there were few things she held back—so why was she acting so timid?

"'Tis your suitor," Angela announced. "I must confess we're all worried about what the future holds." Angela slumped on the corner of my bed, picking at her fingers. "I know you probably view this condition to wed as another burdensome task, and rightfully 'tis a mighty responsibility, but we're afraid you won't choose in time and if you don't choose, then what? What will happen if Tremore inherits the castle and he dismisses all of us?"

"Angela O'Doolan!" I marched over to her side. "Do you think for one moment that those thoughts have not crossed my mind?" I cupped my hands over hers. "Know this, I will not allow this castle to fall into ruin." I didn't dare let on about my concern for the financial state of Kings Castle. "I understand my responsibility and I accept it," I said affirming Angela's question.

"But . . . what are you going to do?"

"I'll tell you what I'm going to do." I took a deep breath, sensing that irrevocable lump in my throat. A handful of thoughts swirled in my mind, and I didn't want to cry, but the layered complexity to Angela's question caught me off guard. I thought about it for a moment, fighting back the tears filling my eyes. I was going to confront O'Riley's financial discrepancy. I was going to reinstate the failing Fair Day program. I was going to do something to help George and his people. I was going to, yes, I would find a suitor, God willing. It's funny how my dream of attending the Herbert School of Music seemed like the fading glow of a firefly at night—short intervals of light and hope and then, poof, the dream dissolved with darkness. This was one area of my life, I dreaded, I was incapable of changing.

"Listen, Angela, all I can tell you is that I promise to put forth every bit of my strength to maintain what we have. I don't want to lose the castle, either. I will seek to find a suitor. Not out of desperation, no! Rather, I will seek to find a strong, suitable companion." I brushed Angela's hand. "I've learned my inheritance is so much more than what meets the eye. I'm hoping you will choose to see this too. And no matter what happens," I pointed up, "His love for us is unfailing and cannot be taken away."

Angela wiped a tear from her cheek, "I know, sometimes my view becomes clouded with worry. You're right, Nora. I think I needed to hear you tell me in your own words that everything will be all right!" Angela appeared to elevate with relief.

"So, what's this about Tremore and his proposal to you?"

"Yeah." I laughed. "I'm not going to marry Tremore! He is not well suited for me. Or this castle. If only Pop knew . . . Now that I think about it, he isn't suited to belong in this county! I only need the strength to tell him—" Angela and I burst out in laughter. Everything would be okay; at least it felt that way with Angela by my side.

The sound of rapping upon the door caused our giggling to subside. As the door pushed open, I saw Miss Celia, Mag O'Sheen, and Mary Ellen McCourt topple into the room. Each of them was carrying a bag or an item of clothing in her hands.

"You girls sure look as though you're having a good time," Miss Celia remarked as she bustled around the room.

"Couldn't wait for us to join ya, aye?" Mag commented as she maneuvered around my keep, placing her tote up on the desk. "Let's get started, shall we?" Mag moved my desk chair to the center of the room and patted the seat.

"I don't understand what all the fuss is about. Shouldn't I be myself?" I walked over and took a seat in the chair.

"Goodness, of course you should be yourself." Mag groaned and I watched as she retrieved a nail file from her tote.

"I don't think for one moment that you'll compromise yer true nature," Miss Celia exchanged. "However, keep in mind that a proper lady must always strive toward making the very best impression."

After everything I'd been through with Albert Edward, I wasn't too concerned with making a proper impression.

"I suppose," I agreed. It was easier to submit to the formalities, as I was clearly outnumbered. I stretched my arm, handing Miss Celia the letters I'd selected from the bunch.

"What's this?" Miss Celia asked with her straight-laced expression turning into a smile. By the look on her face, I think she realized the answer to her question.

"If you would please . . . um, find out if either of these men would accept an invitation to dinner at the castle," I said. At this, Mag made a sound, it wasn't a squeal . . . it was more like the trill of excitement after taking the first bite of a savory meal.

"Very well, indeed! I will send forth a post, first thing."

I nodded in agreement as Mag and Mary Ellen came and flanked my sides. As they worked to manicure my hands, I felt like a scarecrow with my arms spread wide.

"What do you suppose we should do about the others?" Miss Celia asked.

"The others?"

"The other requests, my lady."

"I've decided to forgo the others."

Miss Celia's neck braced up and her lips pursed, again. The same line of worry I'd witnessed across Angela's brow was now on display in Miss Celia. How could I possibly bring assurance to everyone? I wish there was an easier way to explain my feelings, but I would not let them down . . . I would not.

"Miss Celia, I understand that you are concerned for the future of the castle, but I implore you to trust me. I am not a little girl anymore. I have changed, and you said you believed in me. I am capable of doing the right thing, for all of us."

Miss Celia looked at me for a long moment, her eyes bouncing back and forth in contemplation, and then she nodded, affirming her silent resolution.

After my manicure was complete, Mag requested to apply a new brand of hair polish on my hair. She swore by its effectiveness and said it'd work wonders to help tame the frizzes. I obliged her request, anything to calm my wild mane.

We spent the afternoon determining wardrobe options for the upcoming gatherings. Mag styled my hair, suggesting the sappy-looking shine would subside after I slept on it. I hoped she was correct because right now I looked like a wet cat. Once the beauty treatments were complete, the women gathered their belongings and departed for home.

Leo waved to me from across the courtyard. He was leaning against the gatehouse. As I walked toward him, I was careful to keep the financial ledger concealed inside my coat.

"Hey, kid. What happened to your hair?" He raised an eyebrow in question.

"Don't ask." I tugged on the ribbons of my hat, trying to hide Mag's hideous experiment gone wrong.

"All right." Leo shrugged. "Did you look through the book I gave you?"

"Indeed, I did." I reached for the ledger tucked beneath my arm and offered it to Leo as though I were serving him something decadent from a tray.

"Geez!" Leo fumbled with his hands as he scurried to hide the book within the fold of his uniform. "What are you doing?" Leo ducked, sweeping his head side to side, checking to see if anyone took notice. "Do you want O'Riley to discover that you know what he's up to?"

"Actually, yes, I do!" I stamped my foot to the ground.

Leo's eyes bulged. "So, what did you make of those certain . . . transactions?"

"You mean, the payments to T.G. Musical Academy?" I folded my arms, feeling my lip puff out. "You know who has been receiving the funds, don't you?"

Leo's dimple hollowed and his fists clenched. "I'm fully aware who is profiting! With all due respect, I know this Tree Man is your cousin but . . . the back-handed nerve!"

As I listened to Leo rant about the injustice being done to the castle's finances, I felt my mouth drop a wee bit in awe. Why did he care so much about Kings Castle?

"What's the bother?" Leo waved his hand in front of my frozen stare.

"I don't . . . em, I guess I'm just wondering why you would go to all the trouble? First, with Thomas, then Tremore, and now O'Riley. I mean, why do you even care?" Unless I'd misunderstood the ranking system, I didn't see how any of Leo's efforts would make him any more prosperous.

"This is about standing up for what's right. I love this castle. I care about its legacy. And I care about you, Honora Gallagher."

"What did you say?"

"I said, this is about standing—"

"Nae. What did you call me?"

"Oh, that." Leo shuffled his feet. "I guess you could say I called you by your God-given name. So, what do you think you're going to do about the ledger?"

"Well, I feel like marching up to O'Riley and demanding answers but I'm thinking through the best approach."

I couldn't stop looking at Leo's face. Through the years, Leo O'Donnell had been a constant friend. The honorable way he carried himself, his vigor for working hard, and his concern for me gave me a deep sense of gratitude.

"Sadly, until we can clear the matter, I don't think O'Riley should be trusted," Leo said. "His deliberate effort to rob the castle of funds and eliminate your father's desire to give to those in need appears to be rather calculated. I hate to say it, but I fear that he and Tree Man are working together."

"Leo?" I bit my lip, feeling compelled to tell him about my trip to Moore Island. "Do you want to know what happened on my voyage?"

"Life opens bright, kid. I want to hear everything." Leo's eyes sparkled.

I told him everything, including my desire to help George, Anthony, and Maeve. I wanted to make a difference in their lives and I knew what I wanted to give them, I just didn't know how to make it happen.

CHAPTER 16

DAVID ELLISON GREETED ME IN the entryway of the Abbey Hotel.

"Excuse me, Mr. Ellison. I'm wondering if Tremore Gallagher is available this evening? That is, if he's still hanging his hat at the Abbey?"

"Why, yes, my lady, he is!" Mr. Ellison looked over his shoulder. "He is currently . . . " Mr. Ellison glanced down the hallway, "I believe he is finishing up a conversation. Would you like to have a seat and I'll have Shannon fetch ya some tea?" He pointed to a tall wingback chair inside the sitting room.

"Yes, sir. That'd be grand." He took my coat and satchel and hung them on the coat rack. Alone in the sitting room, I could hear faint voices down the hall. Who was that? The voice sounded familiar. Ach! Yes, surely it was Tremore. But the other voice was familiar too? It was too faint to distinguish. Then a flirty cackle burst out down the hall. *Oh. A woman . . . and not just any woman but Violet Ellison. I should have known better.* I felt myself begin to stir with restlessness. Perhaps this was a bad idea. But before I had a chance to gather my things and leave, Tremore emerged from around the corner.

"Ah, Nora Gallagher? Ain't you a sight for sore eyes." Tremore turned, allowing Violet to enter the room before him.

"What a coincidence, we were just talking about you." Tremore winked at Violet.

I swallowed hard. "Really, well . . . " My voice seemed to make different sounds as it came out. "I won't keep you. I . . . em, Tremore, I was hoping I could have a private word with you."

Shannon Ellison entered the sitting room with tea. She curtseyed, "I have some tea for—" and then her eyes bounced between the three of us, picking up on the tension in the room. After placing the tray on the end table she said, "Violet, I could use your help in the kitchen."

"Yes, Mam. I'll be right there." Violet blinked slowly up at Tremore. Her eyes seemed to dance around his face. She took one step backwards, attempting to leave the room, but caught her skirt on the heel of her shoe. If Tremore hadn't scooped her up by her waist, she would have toppled onto her bustle. *At least it displaced that lovesick trance from her face.*

Violet turned to me, "Have a good evening, Nora." She smiled as she left the room. *Did someone stoke the fire because the room seemed to be heating up fast.* I felt sick to my stomach.

"Are you feeling warm?" I tugged on the collar of my shirt. "Do ya mind if we take our conversation outdoors? Perhaps we could go for a stroll?"

"That's a grand idea." Tremore helped me slip into my coat and grabbed an umbrella.

Once outside I said, "Violet Ellison is quite the—"

"She is a delight, isn't she?" Tremore smirked. "But let's talk about you. To what do I owe the honor of your presence this evening?" A slight drizzle began to mist over our faces and Tremore engaged the umbrella, lifting it over our heads as we walked. "Have you come to accept my proposal?"

I felt my face flush. My plan to escape the heat by going outdoors proved futile.

"Tremore, I have sought you out because I need an explanation." I stopped walking and turned to face him. "What is T.G. Musical Academy?"

Tremore devoured me with his dark eyes. He took a sip of breath and exhaled with a slight moan. "Ah . . . " His voice low, and cool. "Yes. T.G. Musical Academy is my foundation."

I felt as though someone punched me in the gut. It was as I'd suspected; Tremore Gallagher was accepting money from the castle!

"Tell me," I felt my words pushing through clenched teeth, "What exactly does your foundation do?" If steam could billow from my ears, surely it would power the next rail car clear to Dublin.

"We accomplish all sorts of things. For instance, we strive to promote artists and musicians all over Ireland."

"So you *have* been accepting funds from the castle?"

"Ya know, I'm indebted to your Pop. He was a man who was inspired by music and from what I ascertain, 'tis the legacy he desired to pass on. I'm only grateful he chose our foundation to carry out his wishes." Tremore winked, and I felt my whole body surge with a strength I'd never known.

"You are a liar!" I gasped. "My Pop would never have replaced giving to those in need over promoting the musical aspirations of an artist. *Never*! Sure, he loved music and that is most certainly the legacy that he has passed onto me, but, Pop had his priorities in order. He would not have wanted the needs of his community to be shoved aside." The words gushing from my lips caused my knees to give way and I felt my vision blur. My exasperation with Tremore's motive seemed to swirl in a wide circle and land with a convicting blow to my own heart. Suddenly, I realized the way I'd put my own ambitions before the castle. I felt my shoulders slink into my back. Still, I was consumed with anger with Tremore for what he'd done.

"Did my father even know about this financial exchange?" I worked in vain to lower my voice. "How could you, Tremore? Especially at a time like this, knowing the conditions we've all been placed under."

"Nora Gallagher, try to keep calm. You are in the public presence after all," Tremore hushed.

"I will not keep calm." My tone spiked. "I don't know what plans you've instilled into O'Riley's mind, but, know this Tremore, I *will* get to the bottom of it and you can expect funding to your little academy to be stopped immediately." I shouldn't have, but I was so mad. I stomped on Tremore's foot as hard as I could, and then I dipped out from under the umbrella and began to march away. Stopping, I spun around and shouted, "As for your proposal, Tremore Gallagher, I wouldn't marry you if my life depended upon it!"

"Mr. Cooper! I'm absolutely delighted to see you standing on your own two feet again." I pressed my hand to my heart. "That was quite the sickness, aye."

"I've never experienced anything quite like it. I, too, am grateful to have come out of that wretched illness. Nonetheless, it's a joy to be in your presence today."

"Shall we . . .?" I turned and extended my hand toward the prepared table. Dinner for two. Albert Edward pulled out my seat, and then rounded the table to sit across from me. He looked the regal part and always conducted himself in the manner of his fortune; yet, he certainly possessed the most eccentric quality of any man that I'd ever met.

Miss Pavek entered the room carrying a pot of hot tea. She tip-toed around the table and filled our cups. She announced, "Dinner will be served momentarily, my lady."

"Thank you, Miss Pavek." I took a sip of my tea, and as I looked up, I noticed Albert Edward form a slow smile.

"What is it?" I said patting my neck and then my face.

"I'm just admiring your beauty."

"I'm not one who receives compliments well, but thank you." I sighed. I was still feeling the weight of my exchange with Tremore.

"You look dejected. What seems to bother you today?"

I felt my back stiffen up. *Was my worry that visible?*

"Oh. Well, it's been a heart-wrenching couple of days." I contemplated how much I should share with Albert Edward but when I looked up, I could see the most sincere expression filling his eyes. Perhaps, he might give me some advice.

"Do you wish to share your concern with me?"

"It's the state of our financial affairs. It's pretty dire." I leaned forward. "Our Fair Day program's been halted and I discovered that our constable is involved in the misappropriation of castle funds."

"You mean, stealing?"

"I suppose you could say that."

"Now we're talking!" Albert Edward squealed in laughter.

"Excuse me?"

"He's a thief. Something I'm familiar with, remember? You know that I can help you?"

This conversation was growing more bizarre. "You can?"

"Indeed! Your financial outlook may appear bleak, but I assure you that there's nothing a little world trade cannot handle. Think, Nora. You come from a family of means. Surely, you must have something in your home of value that you'd be willing to part with." I watched Albert Edward's eyes as he scanned the room, stopping to stare upon the mantel.

Lover.

My breath slowly escaped.

Just then the kitchen door swung open and Miss Pavek stepped into the great room, carrying a tray of food. She placed a steaming plate of fried salmon and smashed potatoes in front of Albert Edward and he said to me, "You know I have a trade merchant who would be able to find a purchaser."

I pressed my finger to my lips attempting to make Albert Edward aware that he should be quiet around the servants. I sat upright as Miss Pavek delivered my meal. After refilling our cups, she retreated to the kitchen.

And then it came to me, an idea. The thought of it made me wince in pain, as it was a horrible thought, but I could see no other way. Albert Edward was right; 'tis the only way to save Kings Castle from ruin. I looked up at the mantel, her rightful place, and two awful words came to mind: good-bye, Lover.

CHAPTER 17

AND SO, IT WENT . . .

An evening dinner with George O'Hagan, the county Chancellor.

A night of dancing with the Viscount Donahue of Limerick.

Taking in a theatrical production with Sir William McCormick.

And so, it went . . .

CHAPTER 18

I'D DECIDED TO TRADE LOVER. It was the only way, as far as I could conceive, to save the castle from further financial ruin. A month after the initial agreement was made, Albert Edward returned to Donegal Town. We agreed to meet at the old pier to make the exchange; I'd give up our beloved fiddle with the hope that Albert Edward would deliver on his promise to trade Lover at a fair price so that Kings Castle could return to a state of financial prosperity.

"Are you sure about this, my lady?" Albert Edward's cheeks pouted. "You know, you don't have to do this. We could find another way. Perhaps, I could arrange to have my father purchase . . . "

"Nae, Albert. I feel as though this way is proper and upstanding." I looked down at my fingers curled through the handle of the wooden case. "'Tis the right thing to do."

"Very well." Albert Edward exhaled, leaning forward as he slid the case from the palm of my hand.

Ach! I pray I've not failed you, Pop. How could I expect Albert to understand? I looked away from him.

"So, this is good-bye. I mean, until . . . " Albert Edward tugged on the brim of his hat.

I held out my hand to bid farewell, and the glimmer caught my eye. I suppose it would take some time to adjust to seeing a ring on my finger.

"Until . . . our wedding day." I bowed my head.

Albert kissed the top of my hand.

I would marry Albert Edward Cooper, son of Ireland's Lord Lieutenant. The date was set for the twentieth of March 1881, a few weeks after my eighteenth birthday and just in time to accept the terms of my condition to wed within the appropriate time. Oh, it wouldn't be so bad. In the time I'd spent getting to know Albert Edward, he seemed to be a kind and decent man in spite of his . . . interesting sense of humor. Surely, together we'd do good work. I felt confident that I could learn to love him.

"Once the trade is complete, I promise to wire the funds straightaway so you can replenish the castle account. Sound fair?"

"Albert." I hesitated, thinking about my words. "Please make every effort to trade her as far away as possible." I stared at Lover cradled in his hand. "I know it probably sounds absurd to you, but there are so many memories. You know I'd hoped . . . anyway," I swatted the air as if a bumblebee were buzzing overhead, "What I'm trying to say is that I don't think my heart could bear witness to seeing her played in these parts." The thought made my stomach do somersaults.

"I understand, my lady." Albert Edward lifted his chin and a sympathetic smile crossed his face. "I shall do my best." Then he turned, walked across the boardwalk, and rounded the corner to the hitching post.

After he left, I sat down at the edge of the dock and let my feet dangle. It was finished. I knew that the choice to sell Lover and my decision to marry Albert Edward would be for the best, even if I couldn't see it, yet.

God, give me eyes to see Your goodness in this.

A hand touched my shoulder and I jumped. I twisted around to see a figure standing overhead.

"Jack?" My back perked up.

"May I?" He pointed to the open space next to me.

I patted the ground. "I've missed seeing you around, Jack. So much has changed since our trip to Moore Island." I couldn't help but stare at him in wonderment.

Jack kept his focus on the streaming river below. His quiet demeanor never faltered. "I just passed by our friend, Mr. Cooper."

"Oh . . ." I felt my whole body sink. Surely, Jack would be disappointed in me as he enjoyed Lover as much as I did.

"I see what you've done," he said, "and I think you've done a very noble thing." Jack turned, looking me in the eyes.

What? Wait. He wasn't upset with me? How could he possibly consider this act . . . noble?

"Oh, Jack." Tears streamed down my face. "I prayed that somehow I could keep her, that even after all the suffering produced by this year that I could hold onto the one thing I had left." I shook my head. "You know, music was the only thing I'd ever really imagined for my life."

"I know, my lady." Jack put an arm around my shoulder and hugged me like a father. "Today, in a sense, you laid down your life. You sold the very possession that's mattered most to you. You did this of your own free will. You made this sacrificial choice. In part, it reminds me of Jesus."

"Jesus?"

"Aye. You know He is our greatest example of sacrifice, laying down His own life for our sins so that we can enter into His Father's Kingdom. It pained him, too. But He trusted that God's will was greater. Following this example of sacrifice in our own lives causes deep pain. It's never easy to let go of the things we hold so dear."

I closed my eyes, still feeling the warmth of Jack's embrace. I suppose I'd never thought of it that way before: that selling Lover was like laying down my life. In a way, it conjured up those similar feelings of death. I felt my shoulders relax as I took a deep breath.

"What you've done has proven yourself honorable, a light for others to see. Thus, you are distinguished, set apart, and have shown yourself to possess a beautiful and moral excellence. Your Pop would be proud of you."

Jack's words gave me a sense of peace within. *Now, if only the others would convey the same sentiments when they heard the news of my engagement.*

"You bloody did what?"

I'd never seen Leo so mad in all my life.

"Shhh. You're going to startle the others." I looked over my shoulder across the dimly lit courtyard. "Let's continue this conversation inside, all right?" I nudged Leo toward the door of the gatehouse.

Leo huffed. Turning on his heels, he whipped the door open, holding it as I stepped in. He wouldn't even make eye contact with me! Stomping over to the gun cabinet in the corner of the room, he pulled out a small tin box and began clawing at the lid with his shaking hands.

"Leo?" I kept my voice calm. "I'm afraid I've never quite seen you in this state."

"Never mind me. I'll be fine!" Popping the lid, Leo fumbled to remove a fat cigar from the box. *What was he doing?*

"You don't understand. I had no other choice . . . " Well, I did have a choice. But I knew deep down that this was what was best for the castle. It surprised me that Leo didn't see it that way. "I had to sell her!" In part, I understood his anger. Really, I did. But down by the river, as Jack assured me, I felt something release in me and I was truly at peace with my decision.

I watched sparks fly in the air as Leo struck a match on a block of charcoal. His first attempt to light the cigar failed. After a few repeated tries, he succeeded. I watched in astonishment as he put the stogie in his mouth and sucked hard.

"What about your plan?" He demanded, coughing. "I mean, your dream. You're going to throw it all away, for what? I'm sure there has to be another way. Why didn't you talk with me first? I never should have showed you the ledger."

"Ach! Leo." I clasped my hands together, feeling my engagement ring on my finger. "You're right. I did have a plan." I took a cautious step toward him. "But neither of us ever expected that life would turn out this way either. Yes, I wanted to pursue schooling in music but . . . I guess God has a different idea. I know it's hard. It was hard for me to come to the conclusion too. I chose to let Lover go because I realized that my real treasure is right here, with you, and all the others. I'm trusting that this way is greater than my best laid plan." Leo's arms hung at his sides, the cigar dangling between his fingers. I took a step forward and reached out my hand to him.

Leo's eyes landed on my hand and I watched the color in his face drain faster than the tide on a full moon. He winced; then as if he'd taken a mighty blow he stumbled backwards a few steps. *He'd seen my ring.* I opened my mouth to speak, to explain everything, but the words would not come. Leo cocked his head and swiftly lifted his chin as if he'd heard a voice from above. Then he vigorously tossed his cigar to the ground, stomping his foot to extinguish it. He marched up to me, cupped his hands around my face and kissed me hard. I stiffened, shocked. He pressed his body against mine. His kiss burned with the spicy aroma of tobacco. There was passion in the way he held me—protective and demanding—and yet it made me feel as though no harm would ever become me.

Oh. I gasped.

"Leo." My voice muted and I felt as though I couldn't breathe. *What just happened?*

Leo stepped away from me, wildly shaking his head. "I'm a fool. I'm a fool." He took his hat off and beat it against his hand. This strong, steady man that I'd known nearly my whole life was unraveling before my eyes.

"Leo, listen to me—I can explain."

"No, my lady. I should be banished!"

"Don't talk like that." I took a deep breath. "I'm sorry. I should have come straight out and told you."

"You're sorry." His head hung low. "Ha! I'm the one who ought to be begging you for forgiveness. It's just—" Leo began writhing again. "I don't know why it took me by surprise. I knew this day would come and I thought I was prepared. I was wrong." Leo refused to look at me. "Please! I beg of you—please forgive me!"

Leo was overwrought, and my heart ached. I had no idea trading our family fiddle and the sight of my engagement ring would trigger such a response.

"Of course I forgive you. We should move forward as though this occurrence never happened."

As I returned to my keep, I wished I could take my own advice. But I couldn't stop thinking about Leo.

My legs dangled over the side of the dock as I watched the river rush beneath me. When I stood to leave the old pier, my footing slipped and I began falling through the air. I screamed. My arms flailed and suddenly my whole body submerged into the river. I was sinking, the current pulling me to deeper depths. I rolled and tumbled through the water and was pushed downstream. When my head finally popped up, I gasped for air and frantically looked for something to grab hold of. That's when I noticed the limb of a tree branch briskly floating alongside me. As the river slowed, I reached to grab hold of it. As we moved, the river took a sharp bend and I saw an open embankment. A dirty looking man with dark hair stood on the rugged shoreline, watching me as I floated by. Something about him looked familiar. Suddenly, from behind the sandy burrow, a gleaming man with bulging muscles stepped forth. He, too, was watching me. He waved, calling for me to join him. He said, "Nora, come!" I felt scared. The next thing I knew, I was standing upon the shoreline next to the bright man who called for me to come. He appeared to be hovering above the ground. I watched as he took rope and bound up the dark haired man. Then he turned to me and said, "These things must happen. The time is now. Do not be afraid." And before I knew it, the gleaming man was dragging the bound man away.

I lay in my bed, completely drenched in sweat, my mind reeling from what I'd seen. A dream. Nae, a nightmare! The image of the dark haired man by the river made me tremble. The look on his face while he was being bound . . . wait, his face . . . it couldn't be. Oh, but yes, it absolutely was! Tremore Gallagher, my dreaded cousin. But he was so filthy. Who was this light figured man calling me? The dream felt so real and powerful. I wished I understood what it all meant.

As I entered the great room, both Tremore and O'Riley were awaiting me. I'd issued a request to meet with them, hoping to privately expose my knowledge of their unfavorable transactions. Seeing them together, standing so proud, began to squash my confidence. Now was not the time to show weakness. Perhaps I should have rallied support from the others. Leo would still defend me, I thought.

"Good day, fellas." I felt my shoulders brace. As I approached, I noticed something tucked under O'Riley's arm. It was the castle's financial ledger.

"What do we owe as the reason for such a gathering?" O'Riley probed.

"The reason?" I cleared my throat. "For starters, O'Riley, I'd like you to summon all of the servants for a prompt meeting in the courtyard this afternoon." O'Riley gave Tremore a concerned look. "I have an announcement to make regarding my suitor."

Tremore smirked as he rocked up on his toes.

"Very well." O'Riley paused, "I've been informed that you're concerned with something you may or may not have seen recorded in the ledger." He pulled the black book from the fold of his arm.

"Indeed." I walked over to the window turning my back to them. This was my first major confrontation with O'Riley and it was harder than I imagined. "I'd venture to guess Tremore has shared with you my knowledge of the situation at hand."

"You are correct in your understanding."

I stared at the courtyard below while I contemplated my response. "It's been a great disappointment, O'Riley. Now, because of your actions, we must sacrifice a great deal in order to revive the Fair Day program." A faint snicker arose from behind me but I couldn't tell who it came from. Was I being mocked? Then an unusual feeling came over me. It was a force, like the wind, causing me to twirl around with hurricane speed.

"O'Riley! My father trusted you!" I stomped my foot with justified fury. "I trusted you too!" Images began to swirl in my mind like debris being tossed through the eye of a storm. All of the uninformed meetings and the mysterious relationship with Tremore. "Yes. It's all coming together. You knew the conditions my father had established, didn't you? You knew about Tremore. And you, you didn't believe I was capable, did you?" I paused for breath.

"Now, now!" Tremore interjected. "There's no need to be so upset on such a fine morning. You're grieving, Nora, and sometimes that causes a person to think irrationally. I think it'd be best if you simply got over it and moved on." Tremore's deep voice slowed. "As for the other matter at hand, I've thought it through and you're right. It was insensitive of me to accept such funds, especially at a time like this.

O'Riley and I have discussed the matter and you can be assured that the funding of T.G. Musical Academy will halt immediately."

"You assure me? Well—" *The nerve. Who had given him this authority?* "What a relief! Nae bother, because from this day forward, I shall assume all financial authority!"

O'Riley piped in, "With all due respect, until you fulfill the agreement established by your father prior to his passing—"

"Let me be the one to assure you. I have already chosen a suitor!"

"I knew you'd come around. 'Tis for the very best, my dear. We shall make a great partnership—" Tremore puffed out his chest.

"It's not you, you fool," I said. "I've already told you that I will not marry you. I've chosen Albert Edward Cooper as my suitor."

Tremore took a step back. He looked me up and down, looking closely to the ring on my finger. "Ha! Albert Edward. Is this some sort of joke?" Tremore shrugged. "You can't possibly be serious."

"Oh, I'm very serious!" And I stormed away.

I surveyed the courtyard: the servants were all huddled together and there seemed to be a nervous energy among them. Their eyes were wide and telling of uncertainty. Mag clung to her children. Miss Celia looked stoic. Angela and John stood arm in arm. Even the entire squad of guards arrived in uniform. I spotted Leo, his head held high, yet, I found he wouldn't make eye contact with me. I noticed the gardens, fresh new blooms dancing in brilliant color. *Life opens bright*, I thought of Samuel Lover's poignant words. *Here we were again, a turning of seasons.*

"Today marks a new day," I announced. "A new beginning. And I'm here to tell you that I believe great things are on the horizon. Indeed,

I have selected a proper suitor! Which means, we have a wedding to prepare for!" A few lady servants shrieked with delight, while others appeared with mouths agape, hinged on my next words.

"'Tis the season of disgrace!" Tremore shouted, hard pressed against the castle's stone wall. Miss Celia gasped. Some of the servants spoke in hushed tones.

"Excuse me?"

"You heard me, Nora! This is such a disgrace." Tremore stood taller, addressing the crowd. "Don't let her fool you for one moment. This, child really, with no skills or ability to govern is sure to lead this castle into absolute ruin, if you allow her."

I swallowed hard, feeling contempt for Tremore. *What blasphemy.* "I beg your pardon!"

"Nora." Leo burst through the crowd like a lion ready to devour, "State your position!" he proclaimed. A handful of guards teamed up behind him. I wasn't sure what to do until I recalled my dream from the night before. The image of a tattered Tremore being bound up and hauled away gave me an instant picture. I looked over at Leo and saw his gun was drawn, he was prepared to fight. I turned my head and looked at Tremore, then back to Leo.

"Banish him!"

"You can't do that," Tremore demanded. But it was too late. Leo and the others had their sights set; there would be no escape for Tremore Gallagher. His capture was imminent. "She is making a mistake. Don't you people see? This is absurd. You're making a mistake. You'll see. You'll see when she weds Mr. Cooper. She'll ruin everything!"

With Tremore's abrupt announcement, the entire assembly began rumbling. I searched the crowd to discover O'Riley cowering in the back. The strong, valiant man I'd once trusted with my life was shrinking back. Somewhere along the way, he'd lost himself and traded his allegiance to the castle and put his hope in himself.

Alas, Tremore was cornered. The guards bound his hands behind his back and carried him away through the open cedar gate. Just as I was shown in my dream.

Before the gate closed, O'Riley ran to his horse, mounted, and rode away.

CHAPTER 19

MISS CELIA STEPPED INTO THE great room holding an envelope in the palm of her hand. "Pardon me, my lady. Sorry to disturb yer breakfast."

"Nae bother." I wiped the corners of my mouth with my napkin.

"I suppose congratulations are in order." Miss Celia placed the letter next to my plate.

I cocked my head, feeling bewildered by her statement. "Congratulations?"

"Why, naming yer first castle official is a rather big thing."

Oh. I wondered why it surprised me that news spread in these parts faster than the blight. "Kings Castle's newest constable, Leo O'Donnell, is certainly a fine choice."

I nodded. "I concur, thank you for your confidence."

"It sure feels like things are shaping up around here." Miss Celia hesitated as if she had something more she wanted to say. "I'll leave you to finish. Lord knows, I've got plenty to do today. 'Tis not like we're planning a wedding or anything." Miss Celia grinned and turned to leave the room. She stopped short at the kitchen door, "Well done, Nora. Yer Pop would be proud!"

Miss Celia's statement inflated my heart with a sense of well-being. She was right. Things were taking shape around here, and dare I say that it felt good for a change.

I picked up the letter and ran my fingers across the official seal. A post from the estate of Viceregal Lodge. Over the course of the last month, Albert Edward and I had corresponded quite regularly. Of course, we discussed wedding plans. But more so, I communicated the happenings around the castle, specifically regarding Tremore's banishment and O'Riley's disappearance. I even shared my concern that Thomas had been wrongly accused. The benefit of knowing someone like Albert Edward was his connection with important figures, and he assured me, he offered me his full support. I wondered, though, could this morning's letter be the one confirming the trade of Lover? The thought of it caused my pulse to quicken. What sort of a person would be looking for an heirloom fiddle from County Donegal? Would an amateur or a professional play our fiddle? Oh, but what if she was bought and never played, only to collect dust on a shelf somewhere? I shook away my wanderlust, tore away the seal, and began reading.

> My dearest Nora,
>
> I have some pleasant news to share. I've managed to find a purchaser for your fiddle. Your timing and decision to trade her when you did couldn't have been more perfect! Don't worry. I've honored your request and I'm quite certain you shall not cross paths with your beloved fiddle. For as I write, she is upon a ship sailing to her new home in Vienna, Austria. A composer by the name

> of Victor Herbert, who owns a small music school, is making his orchestral debut. It turns out he was longing for an Irish heirloom fiddle such as Lover. Perhaps, you know Herbert's famous grandfather, Samuel Lover. At any rate, I'm sure you'll agree that the wire to your financial account is beyond favorable. Looking forward to our blessed union.
>
> Sincerely,
>
> Albert Edward

Incredible! Could it be true? *The grandson of Samuel Lover* would be playing Lover in an orchestra, no less! Who could fathom? I read the letter again. The amount of the trade was three times what I had imagined. This would not only revitalize the Fair Day program, but also sustain the castle for years to come. I felt giddy. It was like I had been given the most beautifully wrapped gift. It was true—letting go, though extremely hard, was part of showing me a destiny beyond my greatest imagination. It's not what I'd planned, but in a sense, a part of me was being sent off to music school after all. Surely, God's will was greater than mine.

I skipped across the courtyard to share the exciting news with Leo. As I burst through the gatehouse doors I startled both Leo and Frank who were meeting.

"I'm terribly sorry. Please, pardon me!" I exclaimed. My exuberance was rising like a batch of dough sitting under the warm summer sun—it was hard to contain. Leo looked at me curiously then shook his head. A smile tugged at the corner of his mouth. Things were better between us; at least, it felt that way. After the night Leo boldly kissed me, we never really discussed it again, so it seemed as though we were able to return to some sort of normalcy. Sometimes though, there was a hint in his eyes, a certain look of longing. It was as if he wished to speak freely but was forbidden to do so. It always made me feel conflicted. I wanted to pry, to ask, yet, I feared knowing would be the unraveling of us both. Perhaps, secretly there was a part of me that wondered if there was more to our relationship.

"What's the happy occasion, my lady?" Frank implored.

"Ach! Yes. I've just received the most astonishing news." I couldn't help but squeal. "You're not going to believe this!"

Leo's eyes grew wide as I danced across the room waving Albert Edward's letter in the air.

Stepping toward me, Leo held me by my shoulders. "Why don't you come down from the cloud you're floating on so we can join you? Tell us what this great and joyous news is all about?"

"It's done. She's been traded," I spouted. "And you'll never believe who the purchaser is!"

Leo dropped his arms to his sides, "Really. Um, who?"

"Samuel Lover." I shook my head. "Nae, nae. I mean Samuel Lover's grandson, Victor Herbert. You know, the founder of the Herbert School of Music."

I unfolded the letter and extended it to Leo. When he reached for it, our fingers touched for what seemed to be a lingering moment.

As he read, his dimple faded. "That's great. 'Tis what you wanted, right?"

There it was, the expression that I couldn't place. The letter was promising and bright. Why, then, did Leo suddenly appear so downtrodden?

"Leo. It is great! You know what this means?"

"Yes, I'm aware . . . we can begin the administration of the Fair Day program. Which is precisely one of the items Frank and I were just discussing."

"Oh?"

Frank stepped forward. "I was explaining to Leo that I've recently met a new breeder of Moiled cows. He is local, too. This is great news for us and the program as finding successful breeders at a time like this is difficult."

"Frank, this is inspiring. How many Moiled cows do you believe we could buy from this farmer?"

"Well, that all depends. It's a matter of funding, as you know."

"It doesn't appear that funding will be an issue," Leo sustained, handing the letter back to me.

"There is something else I wish to discuss with the two of you." I wasn't exactly sure how to explain my desires, so I just blurted them out. "It's my new friends. The villagers I met on my voyage to Moore Island. You see, they need our help. Until now, I couldn't conceive of how to do this. But now, all that's changed. I guess . . . I suppose, what I'm requesting is that we arrange to give them the gift of livestock animals. And Frank, with your new connection I think a pair of cows would be most beneficial."

Both Leo and Frank looked at each other curiously.

"All right," Frank commented. "Let me see if I understand you correctly. You'd like to deliver a pair of Moiled cows to these villagers on the island, and you'd like to be able to reinstate the giving of animals here in town at the next Fair Day?"

"Indeed. Yes!"

"All right." Frank cleared his throat. "And who will transport the cows to the island?"

I looked at Frank and shrugged, "Who do you—"

"I will!"

Leo surprised me with his quick announcement.

"I'll need to arrange some things around here, making sure the castle affairs are in order, but yes, I will see to the task."

"Very well," Frank nodded. " I see my work is cut out for me. I shall issue a formal request to the farmer straight away."

"Thank you, Frank. I know Fair Day is only a few weeks away, but I believe everything will work out in our favor."

Frank tipped his hat and scooted out of the gatehouse, leaving Leo and I alone.

I turned around and saw that Leo appeared to be occupying himself with something on his desk. Perhaps, this would be an opportune time to express myself more freely.

"Thank you, Leo. I don't have all the right words . . . "

"For what?"

"Well . . . um, where do I begin?" *Why was my face beginning to flush?*

"I'm simply doing my duty."

"Nae. It's more than that. You didn't have to commit yourself to such a long trek when we could have paid . . . "

"But I want to do this, for you."

There was something about the way Leo spoke that made my skin feel tingly.

"You know . . . " I paused. "We never really discussed it after everything that happened that night. I'm sure it's nothing. It's just . . . I want to be sure you're okay?"

Leo stepped around the side of his desk and placed his hand on the small of my back. His tender green eyes locked with mine and everything seemed to still. My heart chased and I felt as if I'd scaled the side of a mountain and was finally reaping the tight, airless summit view. Leo. He was a picture of fullness. Why did he always make me feel complete? When my eyes wandered with his, I didn't need words to fill the empty spaces.

Leo grabbed a hold of my hands and I could feel his body trembling. He got down on one knee. "Marry me, Honora Gallagher." His lips began to quiver. "Choose me. I know I don't have much in way of possessions or wealth, or even a fancy title, but I can promise to protect you, to care for your every need, and to . . . to love you with my whole heart."

My mouth became dry and I didn't know what to say. There was no use denying my true feelings. But, how could I possibly turn back to the commitment I'd made with Albert Edward? I put my face into my hands. "Leo." My voice hushed. I couldn't look at him. "Leo, I can't. I'm sorry but I can't . . ."

Despite the overcast weather, the square was bustling with activity. I stood under the castle's Fair Day tent and took a deep breath. The explosion of smells varying from fire roasted pork to unwashed masses and their horses overwhelmed me. I looked around the Diamond at the smattering of tents and the congestion of people and their goods. There were cantmen selling used clothing, and farmers proudly displaying barrels of ripe apples and pounds of dillisk from the sea. It was a relief to finally be back. The joy on the faces of families who came to receive their animals filled my heart with gladness. There was so much about this place that reminded me of my childhood.

"Everything all right, my lady?" Frank came up along side me.

"Indeed. I'm simply taking it in. Every bit of it!"

"It is a good feeling, isn't it?" Frank placed his hands on his hips.

"Any word from Leo?" Ever since he left for the island, he was in my constant thoughts and prayers, day and night.

"I'm afraid not, but there's no need to worry though, these things take time. I'm sure you recall." I knew he was right. Traveling by sea, let alone with cargo, was no minor feat. It's always harder being on the waiting end of things, though. I just wanted to know that he was safe. Besides, I was anxious to receive word on the condition of George and the others. I wondered what they thought when they saw the cows. Oh, how I longed to hold George's hand. One day. Someday, I'd be able to make it back.

I felt a strange vibration rise up from the soles of my shoes. I looked up trying to make sense of what was occurring. The sound of horse reins jingled in the air. It sounded almost like a team of . . . or even . . . a cavalry? I turned and witnessed a cloud of dust pluming into the air. It forced me to cover my mouth with my handkerchief. I was, in fact, correct; a team of horses hitched to a full carriage was barreling through town. I felt concerned for the safety of others. *They'd better slow down. It isn't safe to travel at high speeds through town, especially on a day like today.* As the wagon approached our tent, it began to slow until it came to a full halt. It took a few moments for the dust to settle. Then, I heard the carriage door open with a squeak.

"Mr. Cooper?"

The time had come.

CHAPTER 20

I SAT PERFECTLY STILL IN front of my dressing table while Mag secured the final hairpin. I barely recognized my reflected image. Who was this woman with such sleek-styled hair? I carefully slid my fingers across the silken strands and marveled at the tight bun that swirled in auburn hues at the nape of my neck.

I turned my attention to the four smiling figures behind me; Mag, Mary Ellen, Angela, and Miss Celia.

"You see, I told you the hair serum would work. In due time, in due time," Mag boasted and everyone in the room became tickled with laughter.

Today was the day. My wedding day.

"You look stunning," Miss Celia gushed as she passed me a pair of long gloves matching my white satin gown.

"As do you." I wiggled my trembling fingers into their appropriate holes, stretching each glove up my arm; the smooth fabric warmed my prickled skin.

"Now, you mustn't forget . . . " Miss Celia picked up my Bible and placed it on the edge of my bed. "'Tis tradition for a bride to carry her family Bible down the aisle."

"Yes. I will not forget."

"And the flowers, they are already at the church," Miss Celia continued, apparently feeling the need to announce the various items that randomly crossed her mind.

Mag turned to ask Mary Ellen, "Did you see the bouquets?"

Mary Ellen shook her head timidly.

"They are extravagant! Bunches of ivory Burnet Roses, sprigs of purple Foxglove and . . ."

"Now now, Mag!" Miss Celia interrupted. "Let's not ruin the surprise for the bride, shall we?"

Mag shrugged, "They're a sight, let me tell you! Oh, you'll see."

"Are you ready for your veil?" Angela beamed, lifting an elongated box from the corner of the room.

"I am!"

"Okay. Close your eyes."

I covered my eyes, careful to not disturb my hair or makeup. I couldn't wait to see how Angela designed the veil; her handy work always amazed me. She had a knack for making her pieces look as though they'd come straight from a magazine. My chest felt tight, and, suddenly I realized I was holding my breath.

"You can look!"

I opened my eyes and gasped. As expected, it was a work of perfection! A gold tiara glistened with a strand of tiny pearls around the base. The crown was decorated with similar jewels and Limerick lace adorned the dainty headgear. I ran my hand across the fabric and it felt like soft, white down feathers. Angela cautiously lifted it from the box and the elegant lace fell to the floor. I tipped my head and Angela set the crown on top of my head. Of course, Mag assisted, making sure to keep the shape of my hair she'd labored over.

"The veil is layered," Angela explained. I looked over my shoulder as she showed me how the pieces of lace separated. "This top piece will cover your face . . . when the time comes."

I nodded, "It's beautiful, Angela."

"'Tis the best day ever," she said.

"Well ladies, we'd best be going so we can get to our proper seats," Miss Celia directed.

"All right." Miss Celia turned towards me. "Thomas is awaiting in the courtyard. He will escort you to the church in the jaunting car. Even Snow has received a royal grooming, orange blossom crown and all." Miss Celia sighed.

Thomas was back and driving for the castle again—doing what he was meant to do. I was thankful for Albert Edward and his connections; without his superior rank, poor Thomas would likely be held at the convict depot for the rest of his life. Besides, it helped that the garda were able to apprehend O'Riley. His schemes and the evidence stacked against him proved to justify Thomas' release. This time, I was certain we had our man.

Miss Celia lowered her voice. "I'm . . . um . . . " I could see her eyes were beginning to well with tears.

"Not yet, Miss Celia. If you start crying now, I'm afraid we'll all fall like dominos."

"You're right." Miss Celia smiled, reaching for my hands. "I'm so very happy for you." She picked up her handbag and moved for the door while the others said their good-byes.

"Please tell Thomas I shall be right there. I . . . em, need a moment."

"Very well." Miss Celia ushered the others out of the room, closing the door behind her. I couldn't believe this day was finally here. What a difference a year makes. So much had changed in my life. I think I'd come to the realization that my circumstances are never quite the whole picture. There was always more; things I couldn't always see with my own eyes—like the way the kaleidoscope uses light to reflect different pictures. In the same way, trying to look through the lens of God's light has guided me to see beauty in all things.

I heard a slight knock at my door and I assumed one of the ladies forgot something.

"Come in."

A man's hand curled around the door, pushed it open, and stepped over the threshold.

"Jack!" He was the last person I expected to see. He was dressed in a black sack suit and long tie. "What are you doing here?"

"I wouldn't miss this moment for the world."

"Ach! Jack." I hurried to give him a hug. Something about the way he embraced me reminded me of Pop. He was so strong and sure of himself. I bit back tears by blinking hard. There were so many things Jack taught me this year. He helped me to believe in myself and showed me that I am capable of doing great things.

"I've come to bid you farewell."

"Farewell?"

"I'll be traveling again and I'm not sure when I shall return. I know your groom awaits. I was hoping, though, you might be open to one last song."

One last song? What could he possibly mean?

"Jack? Did you forget that I no longer have Lover? I traded her, remember?"

"Yes. I remember." Jack stepped back. Taking my hand, he placed it upon his heart. "You don't need an instrument to make music. The rhythm, the melody, the movement begins here." He thrummed his fingers on top of mine. Jack began moving. When he took a step, I followed. Step, step, turn. Step, step, twirl. I closed my eyes and allowed him to lead. Step, step, turn. We were dancing. The rhythm was like salve upon my heart, soft and healing. His embrace was warm and filling like the golden sun in the peak of summer.

"Your life beckons you," Jack whispered.

As the music in my heart began to fade, I pulled away and looked deep into the eyes of this fatherly figure, my friend. For a moment, we stared at each other in silence. I nodded. Yes, today was the beginning.

I felt Jack's gentle hand reach behind my back and gather up my veil, lifting it to cover my face. "Know this, even though you may not see me, I am always with you."

A peaceful feeling came over me. I put my hand upon my heart; Jack would always be with me, that I knew for sure.

My heart was racing as I stepped inside the tiny foyer of the church. The doors to the congregation remained closed but I could feel the heat pushing through the cracks. Frank had said the pews were overflowing.

"Are you ready?" Frank tipped his hat. Stepping aside, I was overwhelmed with delight when I saw my little page boy, George. He looked dashing in his suit coat and bow tie.

"Why, don't you look handsome," I exclaimed. George's smile lit up the room. As if Leo's safe return from Moore Island wasn't enough, he'd gone and brought George home with him. Leo said he couldn't leave him, nor would George leave his side. So he made up an agreement with Anthony; in exchange for George coming to serve the castle, being trained and educated in the making of a young guard, the castle would promise to send supplies to the island on a regular basis. I wasn't sure I was ready to partake in the raising of a small child, but when I considered the help of Leo and Miss Celia and all the others, I knew that anything was possible. I only needed to believe in myself.

"Ready?" I took a deep breath as the church doors swung open wide.

The entire congregation stood and my heart beat wildly within my chest. The processional song, *Be Thou My Vision,* began playing. I slowly followed George as he walked ahead of me down the aisle. As I looked down the aisle, I saw at the very end, there he was—waiting, like he said he would. I couldn't take my eyes off of him and before I knew it, I was standing directly in front of him.

As I turned to face him, his emerald eyes squinted, and his dimpled smile arose.

Leo, my groom.

EPILOGUE

BEFORE LEO AND I WED, during those days when I was still engaged to Albert Edward and both Leo and Albert Edward had been absent from the castle, I'd taken the time to quiet myself and consider who I'd most like to become. In that process, some of Pop's last words had come to mind: "When I look at you and the young woman you're becoming, I can't help but see her in you."

Surely, I was coming into my own. Indeed Mam was in me; her passion for music will always be a part of my song. I suppose I could see the image of Pop in me too; his renegade mentality pulsed within my veins. In many ways, their pioneering spirit seemed to spill over into my own life. My becoming—the story of my life—was still being fashioned, but when I'd considered the suitor who'd best accompany me on this journey, Leo O'Donnell had conquered the ramparts of my heart.

I could no longer deny my true affection toward Leo. From the day he'd kissed me, I simply could not shake the deep-rooted conviction that seemed to tremble from within. Those feelings had caused me to consider my life and the effort Pop had put forth in order to establish what he called 'the perfect life' for me at Kings Castle.

Pop had established a solid foundation for Kings Castle and I knew that Leo would unswervingly continue to protect and honor the castle's reputation for doing good. But not only the castle, he'd proven to fight for me too. Oh, we'd have to defy the naysayers who would come against the joining of our different social classes, but together I was sure that we could fair well to build upon this so-called 'perfect life.'

This so-called 'perfect life' could not be if not for the Perfect one—the faithful God I'd come to know more perfectly through my sufferings of this past year. The way I'd learned that no matter what becomes of this life, His love is unfailing and will never depart. This is the 'Perfect life' that I believe Pop had been alluding to.

So upon Albert Edward's return, I'd mustered up the courage to share my true feelings with him and call off our marriage. I'd worried that his favor upon me would spoil. He was a kind and good man, and surely we could have proceeded in marriage to one another and created a decent life together, but the truth was that I could never truly love him. Albert Edward had responded with his signature laugh. It was as though the news of our break up was something he'd been privy to . . . perhaps he knew it all along too. Through it all, Albert Edward remained his kind self, committing himself to me in friendship, and as he departed, I captured a sense of relief in the posture of his soft hug.

How could I deny that Leo O'Donnell was my true love? Joining together with the Lover of our souls, we would embark on this life together . . . this journey of becoming one.

DISCUSSION QUESTIONS

1) Honora's affection for her beloved heirloom fiddle, Lover, runs deep. Have you ever prized a possession that holds a special memory?

2) When Honora first learns of her father's tragic death, she repeatedly asks the question 'How can this be?' In your own life, how have you responded to those hurts that seem to swallow you whole?

3) Thinking of Miss Celia in her state of grief and outpouring of confession before Honora, have you ever regretted something you left unsaid to someone and then discovered it was too late? If you were able to confess your true feelings, how did that change your life?

4) After landing upon Moore Island, the childhood memory of fishing evokes in Honora the feeling of being free. Looking back on your own life, can you name a childhood

memory that has brought forth an unsuspecting feeling causing you to see God's hand of faithfulness in your life through the years?

5) When grief consumes us, we can begin to look at our world with a new set of eyes. Life just isn't the same and we begin to measure time and healing with firsts. When Honora visits Moore Island, she finally picks up her beloved fiddle and plays for the first time since her father's death. How have you measured healing in your own life and what sort of 'firsts' have helped you in your journey?

6) In order to save the castle from financial ruin, Honora chooses to sacrifice the one possession that's meant the most to her. This is her process of dying to herself. Name a time when you've faced a similar choice.

7) The definition of becoming is the process of coming to be something. Throughout Honora's story, we see her character soften. The more she learns about God's faithfulness the more we see her becoming more like Him. Share a memory of God's faithfulness to you and what circumstance He used to mold you into His likeness.

ACKNOWLEDGEMENTS

I'll never forget the day I said, I do. All in. My toes buried beneath the hot sand while I watched my children splash without abandon under the summer sun. I'd just swallowed these final words from Anne {Miller} Jackson's book *Permission to Speak Freely,*

> "Somebody is waiting on you to tell your story. To share how you've been rescued. To share how scary it is but how beautiful it is. Someone is waiting for the little ounce of courage that your voice can give them, so they can begin to find their own piece of freedom . . .
>
> So speak. Freely. The world needs you."

As I closed the book in my lap, I committed from that moment to step out in faith and finally write the seedling story that had been deposited upon my heart.

But this is not my personal story. *Good-Bye, Lover* is a work of fiction. I have however included a handful of real-life historical characters such as Charles Worth, Samuel Lover, and Asenath Nicholson. In addition the Mansion House Relief was a real committee established to aid those suffering from the Irish Crisis of 1879–1880.

The Christian message of God's faithfulness to His people was taken from the Scripture found in Isaiah 54. The faith element woven throughout these pages was intended to show God's unfailing love through trials, suffering, and unforseen circumstances. Oh Lord, You know my heart. Above all else, I pray that Your name would be glorified through this story. Thank You for trusting me with it.

I chose Ireland because of its rich heritage. The lush landscape filled with a history of impossible ruin, deep faith, and a bloodline thick with nobility created the perfect setting.

In 2014, my mother and I traveled to this great land. While I was there I discovered my spiritual affection rang true. I experienced a bond of healing between my mother and I while visiting this root land and I will forever hold our endeavor within a sacred chamber in my heart. Thank you, mom, for everything.

They say it takes a village to write a book. It's true.

Aaron Britz, my main man, thank you for the gift of time you've given me to write this book. Thank you for supporting me and loving me through this journey. Your encouragement to keep going and never give up is the reason why this book is alive. I love you more than all the stars in the sky!

Jill Hass, my bestie, thank you for always listening to my ideas, talking me down from the ledge, and cheering me on.

Julie Klassen, Stacy Monson, Jamie Wright, Tanya Larson, Cynthia Ruchti, and all my ACFW friends, your advice and encouragement has carried my through.

Thank you to Sean Kearns with the Donegal School of Traditional Irish Music. Your passion and knowledge of Irish music has made this story richer. I thank God that our paths crossed.

Thank you George from Arranmore. The time spent driving across the island with you was the most delightful of days.

I'm grateful for all the little fairies who delivered goodies to my door during the long, hard writing days. For all the emails, texts, and prayers, I have been forever blessed by each one of you.

Thank you to everyone at Ambassador International for your professionalism and tireless effort to produce a quality story. And Jamie Chavez, my editor. I consider this journey pure joy because of you, or luck . . . but mostly joy! I'm grateful for everything you've done and shown me including the proper way to eat sliced radishes with a lick of butter and dash of salt.

For more information about

Rachel Britz

&

Good-Bye, Lover

please visit:

www.rachelbritz.com
@britzrachel
www.facebook.com/britzrachel

For more information about
AMBASSADOR INTERNATIONAL
please visit:

www.ambassador-international.com
@AmbassadorIntl
www.facebook.com/AmbassadorIntl